TWILIGHT PASSION

"One step closer," Roan commanded softly, and, mesmerized, Analisa obeyed.

With smooth movements his right hand pinned her clasped hands behind her while his left glided across her cheek, her neck, her shoulder, pushing her negligee gently aside, and came to rest against her satiny skin, his index finger teasing the pulse that hammered in her throat . . . and her heart throbbed visibly beneath her cobwebby gown.

"Tell me again that you hate me," he taunted her, his lips close to hers . . .

RANSOMED HEART

SPARKY ASCANI

AVON
PUBLISHERS OF BARD, CAMELOT, DISCUS AND FLARE BOOKS

RANSOMED HEART is an original publication of Avon
Books. This work has never before appeared in book form.

AVON BOOKS
A division of
The Hearst Corporation
959 Eighth Avenue
New York, New York 10019

Copyright © 1983 by Sparky Ascani
Published by arrangement with the author
Library of Congress Catalog Card Number: 82-90539
ISBN: 0-380-83287-9

First Avon Printing, April, 1983

AVON TRADEMARK REG. U. S. PAT. OFF. AND IN OTHER COUN-
TRIES, MARCA REGISTRADA, HECHO EN U. S. A.

Printed in the U. S. A.

WFH 10 9 8 7 6 5 4 3 2 1

TO JOHN
who's always there, ready to pitch in

CHAPTER I

S
HE WAS reed-slim in her avocado eyelet-
embroidered sheath, and the strappy green
heels made her seem much taller than her five
feet six inches. Bronze-gold hair, bright as a chrysan-
themum, hung long and loose to curl about her trim
shoulders, but what drew the eye was the pallor of
her fair skin, emphasizing the vulnerability and
shock in her wide, lichen-green eyes. She passed
quickly beneath the discreet sign that identified the
establishment as *de la Corte's Mother Lode* and into
the cool interior of the store, the purposeful, staccato
clacking of her heels against pavement suddenly absorbed into silence by thick crimson carpet beneath
her feet. She laid the small boxes on the jeweler's
case and demanded briskly, "How much?" Her
hands had been remarkably steady, but now she
clasped them tightly behind her back in an effort to
disguise, if not to still, their sudden violent trembling. This defensive action unconsciously brought
her perfectly formed, well-spaced breasts into sen-
sual focus so that the casual observer, intrigued,
might have missed the character of her face, which
even without its suggestion of strength and compassion would still have been uncommonly beautiful.

She had already obtained an independent appraisal of the sapphire necklace and the sapphire-and-diamond ring, the latter of which she had worn only on her right hand and only on special occasions. "Twenty-five thousand dollars," the insurance specialist had said, so she had known that the pieces were not personally crafted by Roan de la Corte, about whom she had not thought in years. The jewelry had been a remarkable twenty-first birthday gift from her indulgent and apologetic—why did she so often have the feeling lately he was apologizing?—father; and now five months later it was ironically fitting that she should be preparing to give them back to him. Unfortunately, twenty-five thousand dollars was exactly one-half the amount she needed—today. By this time next week, it would constitute an even smaller share. "The interest is a thousand dollars a week," her father had confessed. "But next week there will be no more interest, no more excuses. They're calling in the bet."

She closed her eyes momentarily to shut out the pain of his indiscretion and was unaware that her pink-nailed fingers were now clutching whitely at the plate-glass counter, leaving a visible trail of fear across its crystal brightness. The house, their fairy-tale palace on Phoenix's famed Camelback Mountain, was already double-mortgaged to the chimney tops, as were all three of their local restaurants. She had listened incredulously as her father had explained that in addition both restaurants in Tucson had been sold in order to meet previous gambling obligations. She could, of course, sell her beautiful robin's-egg-blue Continental coupe, but that would bring her no more than another eight thousand dollars—not enough. And anything less than full payment constituted no payment at all; Antone Costenza had made tnat clear.

"You realize I'll have to have some sort of bill of sale to establish clear title," the middle-aged, formally dressed man on the other side of the glass case was saying with nervous decorum.

She opened her eyes abruptly. "They were purchased here. My father gave them to me for my birthday last May."

"Ah well, in that case . . ." His sentence hung unfinished. "The name, please?"

"Avalon. Analisa Avalon." She pronounced it with a broad *A* and a sibilant *S*, *Ahnalissa*, and her voice was as harmonious as the fine, pale features of her triangular face with its tilted nose, curling lashes and pale, generous mouth. "My father's name is Orlando Avalon. He's a personal friend of Guiglo de la Corte."

"If you will excuse me, Miss Avalon," he spoke diffidently, "I will consult with Mr. de la Corte." A shutter had come down over his face, dark as a storm cloud, and as the clerk took the jewels and disappeared down the sound-absorbing corridor, Analisa's grip tightened on the edge of the display case. Inches away, a golden two-inch-high statue of a roan reared from the gleaming glass countertop. She stared at the bone-whiteness of her fingers, forcing them to relax, and then very gently, with the tip of one index finger, pushed at the fighting mount that was a blowup of the Roan de la Corte engraving that identified the craftsmanship of the world's greatest goldsmith. In spite of its precarious stance on two clearly defined legs, the three-dimensional logo did not move when she increased the pressure of her finger. Invisibly and securely attached from beneath, it was doubtless made of solid gold, as genuine as every-thing else in this elegant salon. Muted gold-satellite light fixtures with five-pointed star globes floated beneath the cathedral ceiling; white linen covered the walls; dark metallic thread was woven through the grey and ivory and mint-colored floral pat-terning of the brocaded chairs. Privileged guests were invited to relax at a Circassian walnut and glass cocktail cube as they handled and appraised and coveted the unique pieces fashioned by the matchless hands of Roan de la Corte. What kind of warring personality lay behind this interior design—everything conservative and pastel except for the flamboyance of the flaming field of red nylon be-neath her feet? Analisa stroked the perfectly formed golden nose of the miniature stallion with uncon-scious sensuality. What would its gold content alone be worth in today's market? How much of her fa-ther's unforgivable debt could be paid by these few ounces of gold, so satiny beneath her touch?

She glanced about quickly, noting that there were no other customers present to witness her humilia-tion, only a freckle-faced young woman dusting in a dustless far corner and watching her surreptitiously. Analisa was glad she would be dealing with Guiglo, the senior de la Corte, rather than with his overpow-ering son. At the thought of Roan, whom Analisa had determinedly forgotten for the better part of three years, two splotches of color invaded her cheeks, a charming improvement over her previous bloodlessness. She wondered, hysterically—because it was better than thinking about her present situation—if she would still be as gauche in his pres-ence as she had been at her graduation dance. How childish she had been then, so instantly infatuated!

And how immature she still was that her heart should beat so breathlessly even now at the mere recollection of his name!

Her nouveau riche father had sponsored the dance at Mountain Shadows Inn for the entire small graduating class of her exclusive private school. If the covert purpose of his sponsorship had been to enable her parents to know exactly where she was and with whom on that notoriously promiscuous night of a teenager's life, Analisa hadn't minded, for she'd always been close and comfortable with her parents and honest enough with herself to admit she was glad they cared enough to watch over her. They themselves had attended a dinner in another room of the inn along with the senior de la Cortes and an elderly couple, Antone and Maria Costenza, who, despite their benign and scrupulous appearance, were reputed, though never legally proven, to be well up in the heirarchy of the local Cosa Nostra. During the course of the evening, Analisa had taken her date, a garrulous and popular football hero from a local public school, to visit briefly with her late-dining parents. While they were seated all together over cocktails—and coffee for the two minors—Roan de la Corte, erect, dark, handsome and mature, had joined them with a stunningly beautiful girl on his arm. Unreasonably, Analisa had taken such an intense dislike to the girl that to this day she couldn't remember her name. Analisa's color had risen, and she had toyed incessantly with her coffee cup, her spoon, her linen napkin, and next to Roan, her own date had paled to insignificance. She had been uncharitably embarrassed for Dave's immaturity, even as she had known, as Roan de la Corte studied her with mocking percipience, that she herself also was being measured and found humiliatingly more child than woman. Looking at his companion's smart satin gown with its daring décolletage and the exquisitely simple ruby dangling from a filigree chain between the blatant curves of her breasts, Analisa had suddenly passionately hated the overstated, little-girl flounces of the yellow gown she had only last week selected with such pride and pleasure.

Roan had the powerful build of an athlete, long-legged, broad-shouldered and lean-hipped, but his hands were those of an artist, poetic in their expressiveness, well manicured with long, supple fingers. She had not been surprised to learn that by age twenty-five, after earning a masters in business, Roan had additionally completed two years of training with Carlo Venturi, world famous master goldsmith of Florence, whose gift of craftsmanship ranked with Fabergé and Cellini. Roan had brushed a lock of hair, black as his own, from his companion's forehead and had murmured, "I get my inspiration from beautiful women, and you, my dear, have me teeming with ideas." He'd leaned very close, lowering his voice to an intimate murmur, but Analisa had heard him say distinctly, "And not all of my best ideas have to do with gold." Analisa had been fascinated by his hands, lean and supple and economical of movement, so sure of what they were doing. Was it possible to fall in love with a man's hands, even while hating the man for the way those hands touched another woman? She hadn't been able to get out of that room fast enough, nor to put Roan de la Corte out of her mind soon enough. In fact, the latter feat had taken months, long after Roan had departed for San Francisco to open a branch store there.

Analisa had grown up in the three and a half years

since that night; she knew she wore her smart clothes to advantage; her life was organized to run smoothly and efficiently, a necessary discipline because of her pressing social and civic commitments. She could handle her numerous escorts with cool confidence or asperity, brittle humor or gentleness, as circumstances dictated. Not since that night when she had fled from Roan de la Corte's unflattering, knowing gaze had she allowed any man to rout her.

The clerk returned. "If you will come with me, Miss Avalon, Mr. de la Corte will see you now."

She followed him at such a nervous pace that twice she clipped his heels. The first time she apologized; the second time she said, "I'm glad Mr. de la Corte is well enough to be back at his desk. I was sorry to hear of his heart attack."

The clerk looked at her oddly, but all he said was, "Through that door, Miss Avalon. Just go right on in. He's expecting you."

"Thank you." She squared her shoulders, lifted her chin, adjusted the strap of her alligator-skin purse and pushed the door open with unnatural vehemence. She stepped into the room. As the door closed, her hands froze on the brass knob at her back and the color drained from her face. Seated motionless and unsmiling behind a huge, uncluttered mahogany desk was Roan de la Corte, imposing in a tailored black business suit with a white silk shirt and a grey tie stuck with a ruby pin. His gleaming black hair waved back to curl above his collar; his was the square-jawed, craggy face of a sportsman rather than the esthetic, fine-featured face of the artisan one would expect. Thinking this, Analisa's gaze automatically sought the elegance of Roan's dexterous hands, but they were out of sight behind the desk—quiet hands that he used to express points, but not excitably as the average Italian does. Unreadable grey eyes, fringed with thick black lashes, assessed the girl. Except for the flickering instant when her eyes had sought his hands, she had moved not a muscle since stepping inside the door.

"So, Miss Avalon, we meet again." There was no definable emotion, not the slightest betrayal of interest in his voice, yet its timbrous sensuality sent a long-forgotten shiver down the center of her spine.

She held her breath a moment to steady her voice. "So you remember the name."

He smiled unexpectedly. "More than the name." His gaze left her face to travel the defensively arched length of her trim, tense body right down to her green kid sandals and back again to her flamboyantly blonde crown. She felt, not unpleasantly, as if she'd been touched, handled. "Ah, that's better. A little color now." His tight smile broadened and his eyes warmed, though almost imperceptibly. "I knew that someday you'd be beautiful, and you haven't altogether disappointed me." And yes, she felt as gauche as she had upon that first encounter more than three years ago. "Come. Sit." With a gesture of one graceful hand, he indicated a chair directly opposite his desk. She made an effort to release the doorknob behind her back, though she was sure without its support her legs would buckle, and walked with deliberate grace to sit before him. She forced her hands to lie loosely in her lap, her head bent in sudden annihilating shame that she should have to beg from this arrogant stranger.

"How old are you now, Miss Avalon?"

"Twenty-one," she answered distinctly, without lifting her head.

"Twenty-one. And still not a woman. Has no man ever made love to you, Analisa?" His voice caressed her, but there was no longer any trace of a smile on his full lips, nor any warmth in his eyes as her head came up abruptly, her face as white and frozen as when she'd stepped through his door.

"I didn't come here to discuss me," she said with ungrammatical tautness. "I came to sell—these." Her hand swept in a graceful arc over the jewels that sat in their respective cases at the center of his desk.

Roan's black brows lifted. "How can you sell what isn't yours, Miss Avalon?"

"But they *are* mine! My father gave them to me last May for my twenty-first birthday."

"May? They should have been emeralds," he said inconsequentially, and then, pushing an open ledgerbook toward her—the only other object on his desk besides her jewels—he added brutally, "Your father paid three thousand dollars down for them five months ago. Not a dime since!" His shrewd eyes watched her. There was not a gasp, not a flicker of muscle as she stared at him in riveted silence. At last she reached out with icy, shaking hands to push the jewels toward him.

"Then you have the right of repossession." Her voice was as frozen as her body. It was time to go, but she couldn't move.

"Are you all right, Analisa?" Sharp concern now, though still no warmth in his voice.

"I'm fine." To her own ears, her voice sounded far off. She wanted to close her eyes, to shut out the hard, autocratic face studying her from across the desk, but it was as if she'd died too suddenly to close them and now it was too late.

Suddenly Roan leaned back in his chair, looking

deceptively relaxed. "How much does your father owe them, Analisa?"

Her dilated eyes widened fractionally. "How did you know? Are you one of them?"

He smiled without warmth. "No, I'm not one of them. I do business with them. Their money spends the same as anyone else's. And the top echelon tend to be very generous toward their wives and daughters—and mistresses."

"But you were there that night, and your parents, with Antone and Maria Costenza—"

"So were you and your parents," he reminded her coldly. "And had you not been otherwise occupied with your own juvenile self-absorption, you'd have caught the undercurrents between your father and Antone Costenza." Then, abruptly, "How much, Analisa?"

"Fifty thousand dollars. This week."

"And next week? Their interest rates are high."

"Next week they're calling in their debt. It will no longer be a matter of additional interest."

"And what are you prepared to do to save him? Or is he not worth saving?"

"He is! He's kind and generous and loving—and . . . foolish. I had no idea . . . He's devoted his life to me. I'd mortgage my soul to the devil to spare him!" Analisa's icy composure cracked. "There's nothing else left to mortgage."

Roan crossed his still hands over his rib cage, his eyes steady and penetrating. After a long, motionless silence, he said, "I'm prepared to pay off your father's folly. But only once."

Briefly Analisa met his eyes hopefully before looking away. "The difference between my share of that

16

jewelry and my father's debt is forty-seven thousand dollars. I have no collateral—"

"You have," he said softly. "You named it yourself. Your soul."

The incredible white shock was back in her bloodless face. "And are you the devil, Mr. de la Corte?"

"I could be." His lips twitched slightly, and there was almost a sparkle of humor in his grey eyes.

"Would I be worth it, Mr. de la Corte?"

"You'd be worth it. I'd see to that."

"How long, Mr. de la Corte?" she asked woodenly. "How would you employ your collateral?"

"Second thoughts, Miss Avalon?"

"I haven't given you my first thoughts yet, Mr. de la Corte," she said fiercely. "I haven't said yes."

He leaned forward carefully, his arms extended across the desk top, hands folded casually. "The men who issue the orders never have to see the results, Miss Avalon; their enforcers who administer the punishment enjoy their work. Quick death is more merciful than acid in a beautiful girl's face or an artist's eyes, or pencils rammed into a musician's ears, or iron tourniquets applied to a dancer's knees. And a more lethal hold on the debtor than his own life is the life of someone he loves."

"No!" The single word was wrung from her in an anguished cry. It had never occurred to Analisa that she might be in danger. But why was he saying these things? Whose side was he really on? With icy fury she snapped, "Are you threatening me, Mr. de la Corte?"

"No, Analisa, I'm not threatening you." He passed a hand wearily across his face, and for the first time she was aware of pained concern in his hard, implacable countenance. "I'm merely warning you." After a long minute's silence, he added, "Have you never wondered about your mother's death?"

The anger in her moss-green eyes turned to terror. "It was an *accident,* Mr. de la Corte. An auto-pedestrian accident—" She stared at him, horrified, transfixed.

"Was it?" he asked quietly, and beneath the fine planes of his rugged face a nerve contracted sharply near his cheekbone. "You may be right. I've always wondered. It happened so soon after that dinner meeting at the Inn. Ask your father."

Analisa rose quickly, gripping her green reptile bag, and he stood as she did, resting his weight on his hands, palms flat, those extraordinary fingers splayed against the gleaming mahogany desk. "I'll be here until six if you change your mind," he said purposefully as she let herself out.

CHAPTER 2

IT WAS that hottest hour of the day preceding sundown—even in mid-October the Arizona sun could be merciless—but Analisa, backing away from the curb and exiting with screeching tires from Scottsdale's Fifth Avenue shops, was too preoccupied to notice. Roan de la Corte's implication was inadmissible. He could rot in hell before she would distress her father with any such preposterous accusation! She now hated the man as intensely as she had once adolescently dreamed of his masterful possession.

Steering between the bristling green-giant sentinels that lined the long drive—"The Avenue of Saguaros," her father liked to call it—she parked directly in front of the wrought iron gate and hurried across the outer courtyard, her heels clacking on the flagstones, to let herself in with her own key rather than disturb the somewhat abrasive cook-housekeeper, who would at this hour be preoccupied with dinner preparations. Only when the door closed behind her, enclosing her in bright, pleasing coolness, did she become aware of the heat she'd left behind. She quickly crossed the expansive, airy foyer, her heels rapping agitatedly upon the turquoise-and rose-colored Mexican tiles. Upon entering the glass-lined hallway that faced outward onto an enclosed desert courtyard complete with splashing fountain and pool, the listening silence of the house suddenly seemed ominous to Analisa's racked nerves. At her father's study, she tapped once, calling with false lightness, "Daddy?" She let herself in without waiting for his invitation and felt an instant's deflation upon discovering he wasn't there. She crossed the room to open the heavy scarlet drapes that were drawn against the late, low-lying sun.

Standing at her father's desk, her hands resting on it in unconscious imitation of Roan's posture in that last glimpse she'd had of him, she studied the wood-framed photo on the desk. The picture had so pleased her father that for Christmas she had asked Tanny's permission to have his original 35mm transparency blown up to this eight-by-ten print. Would she ever look that happy again? She had been dressed grubbily, her usual uniform for working with damaged children—faded jeans, thongs, and cotton floral peasant blouse. Her hair, shorter then, had been tousled by demanding small fingers, her color was high, her eyes and lips caught in a moment of candid delight. Tanny, who years before at age thirteen had been unable to read or write a single word, had even then been a genius with a camera, and he had snapped the shutter in that precise moment when Jody, then as illiterate as Tanny once had been, had read his first complete five-word sentence aloud to Analisa. Thanks to the patient tutelage of Elizabeth Avalon and the school for disabled and disturbed children, Tanny had belatedly been able to graduate from high school at the age of twenty-two. After struggling to establish himself as a free-lance photo-journalist, he had returned to the school that had proved his educability to do a human interest piece on this haven of hope for heretofore hopeless children. Because Elizabeth Avalon had contributed greatly to his personal triumph, Tanny, when asked, had insisted upon making Analisa a gift of the enlargement of the color slide her father had so coveted.

"It's you! It's your mother!" her father had exclaimed upon first seeing the picture. It had accompanied Tanny's article in prestigious *Phoenix Magazine*, and it had brought back to Orlando the memory of Elizabeth as she had looked at a time when they had been unable to afford even the cheapest of snapshots. How many times before her violent death had Elizabeth Avalon returned from her volunteer afternoon at the school with just that joyous expression on her lovely face? That face Analisa would never see again. . . .

Analisa looked about in pained bewilderment. Inevitably her eyes strayed to the pale patches where her father's De Grazias had once hung, barely discernible against the white velvet flocking that covered the walls, for in truth the pictures had not long hung there. Her father had bought them impulsively, more as a compassionate gesture toward a despairing friend than as an investment or from any particular love of art. Her father was nothing if not compassionate, but having purchased the half-dozen pictures, he had come to appreciate them for their native, good-humored vitality. Aging Ted De Grazia had publicly railed and privately agonized over the inheritance tax that would impoverish his middle-class heirs, for the appraisers had set an arbitrary and exorbitant value on his unsold works. His lineage would be incapable of ever meeting the demands of the estate taxes upon his death, so in the end the artist had taken his paintings and his wine out into the Tucson desert and had burned his creations, his children, and had cried and gotten himself riproaring, soul-shattering, mind-bending drunk—but not before Orlando Avalon had purchased and proudly hung some of his finest masterpieces. Analisa had never doubted that her father was a free and generous spender. That he was a driven, reckless gambler she had never guessed.

A deep frown creased her forehead. She had been aware that all the pictures had been removed from this sanctuary where she seldom ventured—but *when* had they gone? After her graduation dance? Before her mother's death beneath the wheels of an unidentified vehicle? What was it Roan had said? "Had you not been otherwise occupied with your own juvenile self-absorption, you'd have caught the undercurrents between your father and Antone Costenza." She had been baffled and surprised, but not particularly concerned, to find her parents in such unconventional company that exhilarating night, for as Roan had callously pointed out, she had been too self-centered to ponder long upon it. And for months afterward she had remained too preoccupied with her hopeless, juvenile daydreams of the dashing, unattainable Roan de la Corte (though in her dreams she always succeeded in attaining him) to think sanely on any subject.

In retrospect it seemed that the pictures had vanished from the walls almost immediately after that dinner. A few weeks later an unlighted vehicle had careened up out of the darkness as her mother had stepped out of the rear door of the Old Mill–Phoenix restaurant. She was dead before she could even cry out, and no one had seen a thing on that moonless night, though half a dozen late diners who had been en route to their cars in the private parking lot claimed to have heard the rapid, perhaps even deliberate acceleration of what sounded to them like a heavy, over-powerful vehicle.

The sudden opening of the door roused Analisa as her father entered, and as if a trap door had suddenly opened in her mind, her unguarded thoughts spilled out. "Then, as now, Costenza called in his bets. But they didn't bring you enough money, did they?" There was no rancor in her soft voice, only hopelessness and fatigue as she gestured toward the empty walls. "So Mama died. And still the debt had to be paid, so you took another mortgage on the house. Or you sold another restaurant. Too late."

"*Dio mio!*" For the first time Analisa looked directly at her father. Beneath the pockmarks of his swarthy skin, his face seemed putty-grey as he sought the support of the nearest chair, a Danish walnut contemporary that looked too dainty to carry his bulk. "In the investigation, there was never the slightest hint—"

"But there was the probability, and you held your silence to protect your enemy so you could . . . could gamble again. And you did gamble again, and lost both the Tucson restaurants. Oh, Daddy, how *could* you?" A tremor was in her voice, but her eyes remained dry and incredulous.

He held up his hands placatingly. "Before you condemn, little one, remember that you have no idea of the horror of poverty and of the contrasting wonder of having money to lavish on those you love, as well as the power to protect your loved ones."

"And what power protected Mama? What power will protect us?" The question was unkind, but imperative.

He held out supplicating, shaking hands, palms upward. "That's cruel, little one. The gambling fever comes on slowly, as pleasantly as warm fire after a long, cold blizzard. When your hands have been frozen, little one, you can hold the flame in your palms without feeling it . . ."

"Daddy, I *do* know what poverty is! Have you forgotten that when I was six years old and all my friends were out playing, I was slaving right alongside you and Mama in that first shabby, smelly restaurant? I was fifteen years old before you expanded and remodeled that one and opened the Scottsdale branch. After that, with one restaurant after another, I guess success just came too suddenly for you to handle." Her father's pained face tore at her heart. "Oh, Daddy, I'm not condemning you. I give you full credit for the uniqueness of design and decor of each Old Mill, for the business acumen that enabled you to finance each new venture. But Mama contributed to your success, too—it was her pastries that put your restaurants on the map to begin with, and *she* didn't turn to gambling!"

Orlando shook his head defeatedly. "It's a sickness, little one. With some people it's alcohol; with others, drugs; with me, gambling. Not just gambling, but money, the headiness of saying 'Name your price' to those who once scorned our penury. I grew up barefoot and ragged and starving in the barrios of south Phoenix. To suddenly have money to spend without having to count and account—"

"Daddy," she interrupted gently, "what are we going to do? Can we sell this house?"

He shrugged heavy shoulders beneath the tautness of his light grey shirt. "Our equity would not begin to cover the second mortgage. We'd still have no money, and we'd have no home either. But your jewels, honey—have you sold them yet?"

"You didn't tell me they aren't paid for, Daddy. Three thousand dollars—that's all they're worth to us."

"Surely you didn't take them back *there* to sell!" he accused furiously.

"Why not? I thought they at least would have pride of product enough to offer us full value."

"Stupido!" He slammed a fist against his open left palm and began pacing the floor. "We'll simply have to take them elsewhere."

Analisa shook her head, trying not to see the fear in her father's face. "Roan de la Corte repossessed them."

"That arrogant young stallion!"

"He was within his rights."

"I'll go to his father. Guiglo is my friend."

"You'll do no such thing! Apparently Guiglo is not sufficiently recovered from his heart attack to return to work; otherwise his son would by now have returned to San Francisco. This is our burden. You're not going to take your troubles to Guiglo and risk his life to save your own!" Her father seemed about to speak, but, his courage failing, he whirled to stare out the window into the early golden twilight of October. With shoulders slumped in defeat, he seemed more a figure of misshapen clay than the cocky pugilist he usually resembled. "It wouldn't have done any good to take them elsewhere," she counseled gently. "Even if we could sell the jewels, we'd still need far more money. And right now all we have left between us is our cars—assuming they're lien-free, of course." She waited for his reaction, and when there was none, she turned and walked from the room.

The city lights winked and blinked in mocking cheerfulness as Analisa pulled up to the curb directly in front of de la Corte's Mother Lode. For a moment she sat in the car, her fingers clenched about the steering wheel. It was a few minutes past six, and already the "Closed" sign hung on the door, but inside Analisa could see the salesclerk removing expensive items from the display window for overnight safekeeping in the vaults, replacing them with pieces of intrinsic loveliness but relatively little value. Even these items "of relatively little value" offered by Roan or Guiglo de la Corte would still be well above the average wallet's power to purchase, for the name de la Corte was known the world over for excellence. Jewelry making, as art and as a commercial enterprise, had passed down from generation to generation in the de la Corte family, reaching superlunary perfection in the hands of Roan de la Corte, whose tiny figure of a rearing horse engraved on the back of any item—a signature he had devised and adopted only a few months ago—could send its price soaring well beyond the cost of any materials incorporated therein.

Unlike many of her peers, who flew off to the winter ski resorts and boated and water-skied their summer days away and danced all night, Analisa sought pleasure in service. It was a concept that had been bred into her from earliest childhood, when her

mother had led her firmly by the tiny hand to visit
and serve the sick, the destitute and the defeated in
the multi-national barrio where they had lived.
Mostly their neighbors were Chicanos and Anglo-
Americans, but there were Italians and Japanese
and Koreans, too; many of them knew not a word of
English, but their smiles, their tears of gratitude
when a bowl of hot soup or a sandwich or a sack of
fruit was thrust into their hands spoke an interna-
tional language. Once when she was very, very
small, Analisa had objected to being taken still hungry from her own table to share her meatless stew
with another child. To her plaintive "Why?" her
mother had gently but firmly explained, "Because
Maria will have no supper at all if you don't share
yours with her. And hungry though you be, you will
survive. Survive. That word begins with 'serve.' I
want you to think about that, little Analisa, always
and all your life, whenever you are tempted to turn
your back on someone hungrier or more destitute
than yourself."

Analisa was thinking about it now as she watched
the salon manager's ritual of settling the Mother
Lode for the night. She had only to agree to serve
Roan de la Corte, and her father would survive. But
serve him in what capacity?

She got out of the car and moved mechanically to
the locked door, unaware that even though she felt
as clumpingly heavy as concrete she moved with natural lissome grace. She was late; perhaps Roan
would already have left. But that was no solution, for
she would then have to humiliate herself by asking
his whereabouts and going in search of him. Before
her hand touched the ornate gold-plated handle, the

door was swung open. "Mr. de la Corte is waiting for you in his workshop, Miss Avalon."

She sucked in her breath, color mounting in her face. She was furious that he should have been so confident of himself—and of her. "His workshop?" she inquired dully.

"Right through his office, Miss Avalon, and then to your left."

She was relieved he didn't offer to lead her, or attempt to follow. What had Roan de la Corte told him? Roan, once the hero of all her silly, reckless dreams, now become the enemy. As she reached the end of the hall, she heard the click of a door, and looking back, she saw that only a single dimmed cluster of stars now illuminated the display room. She was locked alone in this building with Roan de la Corte.

Steeling her resolve she thrust open the door to his office, her eyes automatically seeking and finding the door she had failed to observe earlier. Somehow her feet carried her across the luxurious silver-grey carpeting and to the open door. Roan sat absorbed at his workbench, surrounded by a clutter of miniature anvils and hammers, tongs and engraving tools, in direct contrast to the pristine neatness of his office desk. His suit coat and tie were tossed carelessly aside, his fine-pleated shirt was open at the throat to reveal the black curling hairs of his chest. Rolled-back sleeves revealed arms as disturbingly attractive as those expressive hands. The very room seemed alive with his presence, and Analisa's heart wobbled in her breast a moment before resettling in its concrete tomb. As she reached the doorway and paused, her feet unwilling and unable to carry her farther, he glanced up before rising slowly, to rest his palms again in that eloquent way on the work surface. His carefully controlled features gave away nothing of his thoughts as he watched her with smoky grey eyes, quietly waiting, demanding that the next move be hers.

She stood still as carved stone, fists balled at her sides, more vitally alive than any statue ever sculpted, yet willing herself to feel dead. . . . Her exquisite face was as unrevealing as his as she asked softly, "Are you still buying, Mr. de la Corte?" but her toubled green eyes, unlike his, betrayed shame and entreaty.

"That depends," he murmured, his body as still as hers, but with a controlled stillness unlike her paralyzed immobility of fear. "What are you selling, Miss Avalon?"

Her gentle lips parted, but she could not bring herself to the point of capitulation. "Please don't taunt me, Mr. de la Corte," she begged, her voice vulnerable and gentle.

He moved toward her with the jungle grace of a night hunter seeking its prey. "Taunt you, Analisa?" he mocked gently as one hand lifted with mesmerizing grace to touch her cheek. The fingertips caressed her brow as his thumb sensually teased the lips of her pleading, upturned face. "A businessman always likes to know what he's buying. What are you selling, Analisa Avalon?"

She willed herself not to shatter beneath the impact of his touch. "M-myself," she whispered with only the tiniest quaver, and as her lips parted his thumb slipped between them, so that as they closed, it was as if she offered him a kiss.

"And will you be worth the price, Analisa?"

She wanted to tear herself free of his annihilating touch and flee; she wanted to fling herself against him and plead his mercy. A few damnable tears slid out from between her bronze lashes and coursed silently down her pale cheeks to burn wetly against the thumb that still explored and tantalized her lips. "Y-you said I would be," she whispered, and each word became another kiss bestowed upon his possessing thumb. Her knees felt boneless as fire curled through her, and it was only because she had turned to stone, unassailable by flame, that she was able to remain upright.

His mouth curved in a slight smile. "And do you know exactly what you are doing, Analisa?"

"Yes. No!" A wild light flickered in her eyes, like lightning on a stormy sea. "I'm trying to protect my father."

"No," he said brutally, "you're trying to save your own lovely skin. They want your father alive and healthy and able to raise their money. But you, my beautiful Analisa, mean less than nothing to them."

"My motives—or whatever you believe my motives to be," she argued, "are surely of no importance so long as . . . as I deliver the merchandise on demand."

"Then we have a contract?" His hand slipped to her golden throat to test the pulse there, then moved to tilt her chin as his head descended to hers. She forced herself not to flinch when his lips claimed hers, and when his tongue parted her mouth and sought the sweetness there, she gripped his arms tightly without the slightest notion whether she was clinging to him or fending him off.

He lifted his head to study the misery in her green, defenseless eyes. "A very satisfactory bargain, I think," he murmured, and then, with one arm about her waist, he propelled her into the outer office, still holding her, he seated himself on the corner of his desk and with one hand picked up the phone from its cradle to punch a single, preprogramed button that connected him with Antone Costenza. So his phone had a direct link to the underworld. With dread bordering on terror, Analisa recognized that Roan de la Corte and Antone Costenza were cut from the same bolt, and she had delivered herself neatly into the enemy's hands. But if her father's life were spared, what did it matter?

Her captor said casually into the transmitter, "Cousin Tone, it's all arranged. I'll have your money for you by mid-morning. Just remember, I mean it when I say your doors from now on are closed to Orlando Avalon—and that means all the doors of all your clansmen."

Replacing the phone, he turned back to the girl, imprisoning her in his arms as once again his lips sought hers. Beyond the gleam of pleased triumph in his eyes when he drew back to look at her was a meaning far too deep for her unschooled comprehension. His sensitive fingers teased her jawline, her chin, her mouth—those capable, beautiful hands that could make artistry of raw gold or a woman of a raw girl. As if reading her thoughts, he warned her solemnly—or was it a promise?—"I'm going to make a woman of you, Analisa."

CHAPTER 3

WITHIN the circle of his embrace she stood motionless, still too frightened to react, only the heavy beating of her heart attesting that she was animate. Releasing her, Roan returned to his workroom and began methodically straightening up his bench, locking jewels and precious metals in heavy vaults while Analisa surreptitiously watched every graceful movement of the hard, virile body and the captivating hands. He pressed a button, and upon hearing a smooth, quiet engine sound, Analisa glanced upward to see a metal panel gliding across the ceiling. "To seal the skylight," he explained. "This work requires maximum light, preferably natural daylight whenever possible, thus almost the entire ceiling of this room is glass. When it's closed off, the room is virtually enclosed in steel." De la Corte fashions in jewelry were known the world over; even the cost of the raw metals and uncut stones in this room at any given time must run to the millions, with finished designs increasing their value many times over.

With a feather touch at her elbow, Roan guided Analisa from the room, closing and dead-bolting the massive steel door. Put your car in the employee's parking lot for tonight," he instructed with quiet authority as they left the building, his jacket hanging carelessly from two fingers over his shoulder, the discarded, crumpled tie dangling from one of the pockets. "We'll ride together. While I talk to your father, you pack your things. There's little point delaying your move to my house."

"I—I'm to—l-*live* with you?"

Standing very close, he stared at her, daring her to defy him. "I believe you called it 'delivering the merchandise.'" He ran the knuckles of his right hand down her cheek, the barest mocking smile admitting his pleasure in the feel of her skin.

Forcing her expression to look impassive, she groped in her purse and pulled out her keys. "Perhaps you'd like to move my car for me. Just to ensure I don't try to run away from you."

His self-assured smile broadened as his index finger softly stroked her lips. "You'll not run before the money is paid, Analisa. And I think you'll not run afterward, either. Even if your basic integrity would let you go back on your word, we have a certain feral attraction, you and I, that will bind you to me." She returned his spellbinding stare, but not a muscle stirred, not a flicker of emotion betrayed the fiery, apprehensive tumult within her.

Abruptly she walked away from him, head held high in defiance of the tears that prickled behind her eyes. "Forty-seven thousand dollars is a lot of money for a day girl," he called softly as she slid behind the wheel of her car. Grimly she drove her car around the block to where she found Roan waiting beside his own car. Seated beside him in his flamboyant red

Mercedes she was as rigidly erect as he was relaxed, his calm strength edged with blatant sensuality.

His voice, when he finally ended the taut silence between them, was quiet. "You will completely divorce yourself from your father and his affairs." Analisa gasped softly and drew her knees up sharply, fingers interlocked tightly about them.

"That will be impossible, Mr. de la Corte." Somehow she kept her voice as calm and impersonal as his own.

She sensed his eyes upon her profile for a moment before he returned his attention to the hurtling traffic. "I recall no qualifications to the terms of sale, Miss Avalon," he said harshly.

She resisted the urge to touch his arm and plead, her hands slackening for one moment and then gripping her kneecaps even more tenaciously. "Please understand, Mr. de la Corte, I'm not speaking for myself. I am the only one left who knows the recipes for the pastries, sauces and seasonings that have placed the Old Mills among the finest restaurants in America. Even Daddy doesn't know; he's the organizer, the administrator, invaluable in his services, but goodness knows he can't even open an egg without crushing it. With Mama gone, he's totally dependent upon me to maintain quality in the kitchens."

"I see," Roan conceded thoughtfully after several moments of reflection. "I've often wondered why you continued to work while so many of your peers were at play."

"You were aware that I work?" She felt a strange flutter somewhere inside her.

"I'm aware of a great many things about you, Analisa Avalon," he said mysteriously. She lowered her head, biting her lip in a vain effort to still its trembling. "Obviously we'll have to work out a compromise for the time being. But as quickly as possible, you will have to find someone to whom to entrust your secrets."

For the first time since she had entered the car, Analisa turned her head to look directly at him, her dilated eyes shining as darkly green as a cat's. "Thank you, Mr. de la Corte. May I have a month?" Then, almost to herself, "It's a pity there's no family left."

Parking his car at Analisa's home precisely where she'd earlier left hers, Roan handed her out and guided her through the wrought iron gate. "Leave me alone with your father while you pack," he commanded with his easy authoritative manner as they crossed the foyer. "Be sure to take everything you need, for you'll not be returning to this house."

"I haven't enough cases for everything. I'll have to come back to—"

"I'll arrange to have the rest sent over." Once again he ran his knuckles lightly down her cheek, and she held her breath in an effort to deny the turmoil he created within her. "I'll send your father along to say good-bye to you and give you a few minutes alone with him."

Unable to hold his gaze, she turned her full attention to knocking on the framework surrounding the padded leather door to her father's study. "Daddy?" She swung open the door and peered around it. Her father was slumped in a deep leather chair, legs stretched before him, heels apart, a half-consumed water tumbler of straight whisky clutched in his left hand. "Roan de la Corte is here to see you, Daddy." She stepped aside, and as her escort moved past her into the room she glided silently to a glass sliding door and let herself out, crossing the inner desert courtyard to her own luxurious room at the opposite side of the house.

Because she couldn't take everything, she selected a few representative items from each group—sportswear, day wear, formal dresses—which she had already slipped into dry-cleaning bags for hanging in the rear of the car. She had chosen several pairs of shoes and was cramming toiletries and lingerie into her four-piece matched luggage when her father entered ghost-quiet, his face grey, his poor skin—lasting evidence of dietary deficiencies when he'd been a barrio youngster—rendering him old and leprous-looking. He pressed a hand to his rib cage, directly below his heart, and Analisa crossed the room to him in alarm, reaching out to touch his shoulder with a loving hand. "Daddy, are you ill?"

"Little one, what have I done to you?" He moaned and leaned against the closed door of her nearly empty walk-in closet, burying his face in his hands, and it was several minutes before he composed himself enough to speak. "I can't let you do this, Analisa."

"Nonsense! It's already done!" she said flippantly as she turned away, ostensibly to snap the last lock on her cosmetic case but in truth to conceal from him her own terrible distress.

"But to sell yourself to the enemy—"

Her heart closed like a fist, dealing a hammer blow to her stomach, and she felt her limbs freeze from sudden fear. She herself had asked Roan de la Corte if he was one of them, and he had denied it—though not, she realized in retrospect, with any great emphasis. She whirled to face her father, the anguish showing in her lovely, pure face. Once again he clutched at his heart. "Let them kill me, Analisa, but don't do this to yourself."

"They don't want you dead!" she cried despairingly. "They want you alive to pay your gambling debt. But because I mean everything to you, *I* am the ace up their sleeve—" She stopped, aghast. She had not meant to say that to him.

His hands gripped her shoulders painfully. "Now I begin to understand de la Corte. To protect you, he would make you seem to turn against me and join them. Perhaps he is a better man than I thought, little one. Forty-seven thousand dollars is a lot of money to pay for a mistress. Can it be that, beyond fancying you, he even cares a little?"

Her heart lurched at the possibility, until she recalled her purchaser's cold manner. "No, Daddy. 'Fancies' is the correct and only verb. But what's important to me is the promise he has extracted from Antone Costenza that none of his family will ever again permit you to gamble." An aggrieved expression crossed her father's haggard face, but before he could protest she reminded him gently, "You know you would, Daddy. Nothing has ever stopped you before."

"But don't you think the knowledge that I have sold you into white slavery is enough to cure me?" he whined, and for the first time, Analisa was truly aware of her father's inherent, incurable weakness.

"It's not white slavery!" she protested indignantly. "He's not going to—to pass me around—" But even as she said it, the possibility loomed real. *You'd be worth it. I'd see to that,* he had promised. God in heaven, what had he said to her father? Would Roan make her earn back every cent? The color drained from her cheeks as she hurled herself into her father's arms. "No, Daddy, no! He won't!"

Her father lifted her face. There was so much pity in his bleak eyes that she wanted to cringe from him. "I have to believe that he will. And you have to face reality. You are a lovely child, all the more so to me because you are your mother's reflection in the mirror of my eyes. But Roan de la Corte has a surfeit of beautiful women at his service—wordly, experienced women capable of pleasing every erotic impulse of his virile body. He has no personal need of you, nor of your unbloomed promise of beauty, and I doubt he would have anything but scorn for your innocence."

She pulled away and tossed her head angrily, denying her very real fear, her golden-bright hair swinging about her face and shoulders. "If I believed that, I'd kill myself and let the devil take you. But don't you see, this is what I've wanted, to belong to Roan, ever since I first met him at my graduation dance." Determined only to ease the pain of his conscience, even she didn't suspect as she plunged recklessly on that deep down in her heart might lie the seed of truth. "Daddy, why do you think I could never take seriously any of those foolish young boys you have tried to marry me off to the past three years?"

Her father smiled sheepishly, believing her because he needed to believe. "So the trapper is trapped, eh?" He chuckled softly, and before he could recognize the fear lurking beneath her insouciance she went to her private bathroom to wash away all traces of her tears of shame and terror.

When she returned to the room, her father had gone and Roan was standing in the open doorway, a strange expression on his face. "Is this it, then?" he asked, indicating her cases lined along the floor and the bulging plastic carriers on the bed. She nodded, and together they lifted them to carry them to the car.

Full night was upon them, and as they turned north on Scottsdale Road, leaving the city lights behind, blackness surrounded them. Analisa had expected to be delivered to an apartment complex in town, but instead they were racing silently away from civilization, the automobile headlights startling tiny white kangaroo mice as they bowled across the highway, confusing rabbits that started to cross and then turned to parallel the lights in panicked, suicidal flight.

"Where are you taking me?" Analisa asked when she could bear the tension no longer.

"Home." His fine hands were relaxed on the wheel; hers were gripped tightly in her lap.

"To your parents' home," she amended, overwhelmingly relieved, recalling that some years ago Guiglo de la Corte had built his wife's "dream home" among the jumbled desert rocks of the then newly developing community of Carefree.

Though she didn't look at him, staring straight ahead into the mesmerizing path of the headlights, she was aware of his taunting smile. "At one time it was. Since my father's heart attack they've moved into a town house where the living's less complicated."

"Are you not planning to return to San Francisco then?" She forced her voice to remain conversational, knowing that despite her best efforts, it contained none of its usual animated warmth.

"It remains to be seen. If eventually my father's health permits him to return to work, it's more than likely he'll be the one to take over the San Francisco operation. The Scottsdale workshop is far superior to any I've seen anywhere else in the world, and it would be exorbitantly expensive to duplicate it elsewhere. Meanwhile, we have Trenton Westfield to look after the San Francisco shop until we can find a suitable replacement for him, at which time I plan to bring him here to continue his apprenticeship. He has a rare talent for jewelry design which I'd be a fool not to exploit."

Forgetting her anxieties, she looked at her companion in astonishment. "But shouldn't that apprenticeship be reserved for the next de la Corte?"

His eyes glistened and his teeth gleamed white in his amused glance. "I'm an only child, and I've yet to fall in love. What guarantee do I have that there will ever be another de la Corte?"

"But surely you plan eventually to have a fami—"

"Not even for an heir would I tie myself for life to a woman I didn't love."

"You *are* only twenty-eight!" she said, then flushed in the darkness, impatient with herself for betraying that she had any knowledge of or interest in him. "There's still plenty of time for you to fall in love and marry."

"How clever of you to have done your homework," he jibed, then continued, "A little late at twenty-eight to feel with any certainty that I will ever develop any permanent interest in a woman, yet I'm far too young to anchor my whole life to a shipwrecked marriage."

"Why are you so convinced your marriage would founder?"

"I know my limitations, Analisa. I'm not an easy taskmaster. And women are of a sameness that quickly bores me. I've yet to meet one who feels that how she performs in bed isn't all that matters." He allowed his lips to relax into a wicked smile as one hand moved from the wheel to cover hers in her lap. "By any chance, Miss Avalon, are you proposing marriage to me? Or the propagation of a child without marriage?"

"Certainly not!" She turned quickly away in confusion. "Besides, I haven't the least idea how I would perform in bed. I'm sure I'd be a dismal disappointment."

"Never mind," he consoled teasingly. "Lovemaking, like any other art, can be learned with the proper teacher. And you, I can assure you, will have the very best schooling." With a gasp of resentment, tinged with not unpleasurable fright, she jerked free of his grasp and turned to stare out the side window, her cheeks on fire. After a prolonged silence, he found her staring at him in fascinated entreaty. "Then you aren't planning to—parcel me out." It was a statement because she dared not make it a question.

He laughed softly, a sound deep in his throat that touched upon every nerve in her body. "And why not? I'm in the business of fashioning and selling fine jewels, and what finer jewel in all the world than a beautiful innocent?"

"You're only saying that to tease me, of course," she protested uncertainly, "but it's a cruel joke. You know I have never . . . would never . . ."

"Yes. I know you've never. You are so unmistakably virginal. Beautiful and virginal—how does one put a price tag on a priceless jewel?"

She stared at him silently, her retort caught in the sob that clogged her throat. He returned his attention to the road and after a moment, as if the matter were of the utmost inconsequence, added, "After the first time, it comes easy. There's nothing more to lose." A searching pause. "Tell me, Analisa, what price would you put on your maidenhood?"

"My body is not a piece of merchandise," she protested tartly, "separate from heart and honor and self-respect. The price cannot be calculated in coin, but only in love. . . ." Her voice trailed away as her thoughts turned again to her own grim future.

"Love! What an old-fashioned concept!"

The scorn in his voice stung her; the memory of her father's warning rose to terrify her anew. In revealing the diabolical details of his trade-off, what scheme had this man laid out for Orlando Avalon's enlightenment—this devil who could with a mere glance, a touch, a laugh, stir up hellish fires of need and desire within her?

"I was taught to believe in love and chastity," she remonstrated rather primly. "It served my mother well—"

"Did it?" The words bit into her thoughts, as ugly as teeth into flesh, "In the end, it served her brutal death. But however ill or well it treated her, she is of another generation, when sex and love were said to be inseparable. You are of *this* generation that recognizes sex as a thing apart from love, just as true love—*if* such a thing actually exists—might endure without sex."

"You're illogical and inconsistent, Mr. de la Corte. In one breath you rate purity as a priceless jewel; in the next you scorn it as valueless. I suggest that until you know your own mind you cease your preaching and philosophizing!"

She registered the tightening of his lips, the

smouldering anger in his eyes, and accepted his silence as a strategic, if only temporary, withdrawal from the battle. No further conversation passed between them until the car had been parked on the graveled edge of a natural desert garden lit by footlights that illuminated a pathway to a great carved front door. Roan gathered some of Analisa's things and walked her to the threshold. He unlocked first the ornamental wrought iron grille that protected the door, then the door itself, and ushered her into the marble-floored entrance hall, where a lighted fountain in the center of the foyer gave the only sign of life.

She had not been able to see the house at all until they'd actually left the car. She knew that this home, like all of those in the original Carefree community, would be situated on its own large acreage, carefully blended into its rocky background with neutral colors and harmonious lines so that even in daylight she might have passed it by. Originally by gentleman's agreement and later by proclamation, no home here was allowed to intrude upon its neighbor's eyes or disrupt the tranquility of the natural desert. There had been no sign of gateposts, no elaborate entryway broadcasting the proximity of the house, and had she been driving, Analisa would have missed the turnoff, winding as it did among the paloverde, the ocotillo, saguaros, sage and ephedra, here and there dodging around great beige or grey lichen-dressed boulders.

When the heavy door closed behind them, shutting out the night calls of the desert, the only sound that remained was the chattering of the miniature fountain that served as night-light. At last Analisa spoke.

"Are all the servants gone? Do you have servants?" She couldn't quite suppress an apprehensive shiver.

"Joe and Ardith Hanson come in three days a week to garden and clean. When I expect to dine in, Ardith stays over to prepare dinner. I tend my own breakfast." Depositing onto the floor the case he carried, he leaned forward to remove the light bolero she'd donned against the night chill, his fingers disturbing against her nape. "Are you hungry? I should have suggested dinner in town." He smiled sardonically. "I had other things on my mind."

She stepped gingerly away from him, feeling the continuing shock of forbidden desire his touch aroused. "Show me the kitchen and I'll fix something. I'm not hungry, but I expect you're starved."

He smiled and flicked a long bronze-gold lock back behind her ear. "Not for anything in the kitchen." She backed another step, and his hand curved possessively about her neck. "There's no running, Analisa. I'll show you your room, and then I'll bring in the rest of your cases while you prepare supper. Something light so late in the evening, I should think."

She followed him obediently, her heels echoing on the brilliantly polished black marble underfoot. "Your room," he'd said, not "our room." As he switched on lights ahead of him and entered a white carpeted hallway with oyster-white walls, she halted abruptly to stare up at a painting, both hands clutching the handle of the cosmetic case she carried. Her eyes darted to several more pictures that lined the wall. Her host turned to watch her reaction with mild curiosity. "So this is where my father's pictures went," she murmured. "Your father took his treasured de Grazias and your cousin took his money. And one of you took the life of the only woman he ever loved." She turned to stare at her escort, her abductor, but she didn't really see him, because that other fear she'd tried so hard to subdue, the one that contained none of the disturbing pleasurableness she'd felt only moments ago, rose before her like a spectre, blocking her vision. If she didn't see the anger in his eyes, she at least heard and recognized the impatience in his voice as he grasped her arm and propelled her beside him down the hall.

"I told you, Analisa, I am not one of them. Nor is—or was—my father. Your father needed to make a quick sale of his paintings; my father agreed to buy them, at a price considerably greater than yours originally paid. That it still wasn't enough to cover your father's debt can hardly be attributed to my father's parsimony."

Almost roughly he shoved her through the doorway next to the last on their right, where she paused to survey the room with unexpected delight. Beneath a cathedral ceiling a round bed was casually draped in brilliant apricot. Matching drapes adorned a glass wall and were now drawn aside to reveal gold and white pussy-willow sheers. Underfoot was the same plush white carpeting that lay in the hall, and moving farther into the room she saw that it extended down a smaller hallway into what could only be the master bedroom. Opening off that hall to the right was a master bath, facing which were linen closets with sliding doors. An immense wardrobe with mirrored sliding doors was duplicated, she assumed, by a similar closet in the master bedroom. Against one wall was a built-in white and antique-gold dresser with its own shell-shaped basin at one end and an oval vanity stool skirted in the same apricot velvet as the bedspread and drapes. On each side of the bed was a black nightstand, and against the wall adjacent to the closet, a tall, broad matching chest of drawers.

"It's beautiful!" she gasped. "It makes my lovely room at home seem a hovel."

Roan allowed himself a small smile. "It was my mother's retreat. I'd hoped you would like it."

"I love it!" Then her eyes clouded. "Is there no door between the two rooms?"

"There's a pocket door at each end of the connecting hall." He moved forward to demonstrate, sliding the near one out of the wall. He fixed her with a dark look and added softly, "But they'll not be used. Under any circumstances."

"I—I—of course." Quickly she went to deposit her vanity case on the near nightstand, keeping her back to him. She would not let him see the tears of humiliation in her eyes! She had made a bargain, and he would never know the blow he had dealt to her pride, her independent spirit, and most of all, to her self-respect. "I—of course," she repeated stupidly just as his hands closed over her forearms, turning her so that he could look into her eyes.

"I'm not planning to rape you, Analisa."

"I hadn't imagined you were," she replied drily, regaining, at least outwardly, her cool composure. "If you'll show me the kitchen, Mr. de la Corte . . ."

She had grown up in the kitchen, first as dishwasher and potato peeler, then as after-school waitress and dishwasher, and, by the time she was thirteen, as cook's helper. Preparing dinner in Paris de la Corte's well-organized, cheerful kitchen with its genuine flagstone floor, white cabinets and aqua

Formica countertops did much to restore Analisa's confidence, and by the time Roan was seated opposite her at the breakfast bar she was feeling almost cheerful. With both elbows propped inelegantly on the countertop, she bit into her scrambled egg and mustard sandwich and after a moment commented, "I usually go into each restaurant one day a week to prepare the pastries and sauces."

"I thought all baked goods were prepared fresh daily," he said accusingly, as if he felt he'd been personally duped by false advertising.

"They are," she hastened to explain. "They're *baked* daily, but the mixes are prepared once a week. You see, half the secret is in thoroughly chilling the basic mixes before using them. The other half, of course, is in the combination of ingredients. Spices and seasonings I do only about every three months. Once the basics are done, anyone can complete the product." She hesitated. "I do the mixes for the Tempe restaurant on Tuesdays, and tomorrow is Tuesday."

His grey eyes pierced her. "Tomorrow we have to go to the bank and pay a visit to Cousin Tone."

"Oh. Must I go with you?"

"You must." His decisive tone left no room for argument. After a moment's consideration, he added, "The afternoon will be yours. We have a dinner date at eight tomorrow evening."

It was nearly midnight when he escorted her to her room. "Do you like sleeping beside a running stream?"

"I'm not sure. It sounds delightful."

Crossing the room, he opened the sheers and slid the glass door aside. A muted outside light had been turned on, presumably while she had prepared supper and he had carried in her luggage, and now she could hear the chortling of water on rocks outside her door. She went to stand beside him and gaze in wonder at a small but picturesque waterfall tumbling down the jagged rocks into which the house seemed to be built. "Is it a natural stream?"

"No." She was acutely conscious of his arm about her shoulder as he drew her outside onto a flagstone patio. "It's nothing more than a small, glorified swimming pool. Only the rocks forming the waterfall are natural; the water is recirculated by a pump." The water, crystal clear and pale gold beneath the lights, splashed down from the high tumble of rocks, washing over the clinging greenery of a hanging garden and spilling into an irregular-shaped pool, as natural-looking as any wild pond. There were no steps leading into the water, no diving board to detract from the illusion of a small oasis in its natural state. There were two recliners set out on the flagstones and a round metal table that needed no sun umbrella, since a paloverde growing out of the rock escarpment offered sufficient shade during daylight hours.

"It's fascinating," she murmured. "Dare I sleep with my door open?"

"You do," he smiled. "That's what these wrought iron grilles are for—though even without them, I expect you'd be safe enough out here." He indicated the glass wall of the adjacent room and said, "I close my doors only on the vilest nights, of which there are few."

She smiled impishly and wished her erratically beating heart would behave sensibly. "But of course, you've been here only three months and fall has barely set in. Wait until January and let's see what

48

you have to say. Since you grew up in town, you are probably unaware that the elevation here is just that much higher that a January rain in Scottsdale or Phoenix can become five inches of snow out here."

Returning to her room without comment, he closed and padlocked the iron grille, leaving her door open, then lifted a cobwebby gown she had not noticed draped over the bed. "Wear this."

She flushed angrily. "What right had you to open my cases?"

"Every right," he said curtly, striding to his own room.

She stood frozen, realizing that from now on she had no choice but to do his bidding. Then she fished the matching negligee from her suitcase and raced to lock herself in the bathroom. When she emerged half an hour later, bathed and sweetly scented, her hair brushed to shimmering bronze lights, he was standing at his own end of the short dividing hallway, legs wide, his shirt unbuttoned to reveal the brownness of throat and chest, absently undoing his cuffs as he studied her intently. She had turned off the bathroom light as she exited, leaving only a dim nightlight burning on one of her nightstands, yet she felt acutely conscious of her own silhouette, aware that against the light her nightclothes surely revealed as much as they concealed. She paused an instant in the hallway, as if physically pinned beneath his inscrutable gaze, her lips unconsciously parted in the silent pleading she swore she'd not do, and then she turned and fled to her room, plunging beneath the covers of her bed without even bothering to remove the exquisite velvet spread.

She lay defensively on her stomach, her head buried between the pillows, waiting in trepidation.

She heard him enter the bathroom to shower, come out again, and still she waited. Presently she opened her eyes to find that their rooms were in total darkness. She rolled onto her back and stared into the moonless blackness, listening to the soothing tumble of water outside their adjoining rooms.

He didn't come to her, and after awhile, it occurred to her that a man who meant to sell her virginity to the highest bidder would want no intimate association of his own with her.

CHAPTER 4

ANALISA rolled over with a soft moan of protest as a hand brushed her face, light as a summer breeze, and her eyes flew open as memory returned, sharp and devastating. Roan sat on the rounded edge of the bed, fully clothed. Lying there helplessly, flat on her back in her filmy attire, she automatically pulled the covers tight about her chin. His faint smile seemed friendly.

"A fine cook you turned out to be," he teased her. "We have to be at the bank in an hour, and now there's no time for more than a quick cup of coffee and a slice of toast. Did you sleep well?"

"Yes. No." She jerked the covers up to cover her head, wanting only to return to the safety of oblivion. She remembered how she had lain awake for hours. Once she had gotten up, hugging herself as she shivered in the cold predawn air, and had wandered to her open door to stare into the darkness and listen to the music of the tumbling waters. It had occurred to her then that the iron grille was as much a prison gate as a safeguard. But that was silly, she'd scolded herself; the gate had been installed years ago, when the house had been built, to protect the woman Guiglo de la Corte loved. What would it be like to be loved by a de la Corte? Angry with the turn of her thoughts, she had returned to her bed, properly removing and folding the beautiful spread and the negligee that by then had already been crushed by hours of tossing, and finally she had slept.

Roan was obviously waiting for an explanation, so despite her lethargy and her apprehension she uncovered her head and smiled shyly up at him. "I missed the late movie. Such deep sleep always exhausts me."

"The late night movie?" he said quizzically.

"My REM sleep. A dreamless sleep is never restful, you know. You should have woken me sooner," she accused. "I couldn't be tireder than I am, and at least I'd have cooked you a proper breakfast."

"You looked too beautiful and vulnerable and defenseless lying there. I couldn't bring myself to disturb you."

His remark, however it was intended, only served to remind her of her position. She sat up abruptly, her weight resting back on the heels of her hands. The covers slid down to the upper curve of her breasts, anchored beneath her armpits. "Defenseless!" she spat. "That's the key word, isn't it?" Her head drooped, the long golden curtain of her hair falling forward to shield her vulnerable expression. He sat quietly studying her, until at last she lifted her head to return his gaze. The smallest tremor denied the bravado of her upthrust chin. "I am defenseless," she said, thinking to make him feel guilty, but the soft sadness in her eyes robbed her voice of the stinging contempt she'd meant to deliver. Not even to herself would she confess that all the contrived hatred in the world would be as ineffectual against the power of his magnetism as a needle against the pull of polarized iron.

He moved his face dangerously close to hers, reaching out his hand to stroke her neck and throat thoughtfully. "Virginity always leaves one vulnerable, I think," he murmured. "A virgin—the most precious of man's acquisitions." She remained frozen in place, her mind defying him, her body willing him to kiss her. Suddenly he stood up, snapping the covers to the foot of the bed in a single swift movement, his eyes raking her body, appreciating all the lovely details only slightly muted beneath the diaphanous white gown. "Get up!" he ordered harshly, adding mockingly, "or we shall miss our appointment at the bank and you shall have given yourself to me—*freely*!" His unmistakable emphasis on the last word unfroze her and sent her scurrying for the security of the bathroom.

"Wear something sexy," he ordered, and her head popped back out in astonishment.

"Sexy? At this time of day?"

"Yes, at this time of day," he rejoined grimly as he strode from the room, flinging over his shoulder, "Coffee's made. If you hurry, you'll still have time for a cup."

Analisa had felt that mid-October was too late in the season for a low cut sundress, and anyway, what did Roan mean by "sexy"? Clothes meant different things to different men. She had finally settled on a sea-colored dress that vied between green and blue and accentuated the wide green innocence of her eyes. Though the sweetheart neckline was modest, the fitted waist and slightly gathered bust of the dress emphasized the firm curves of her small breasts, and the shirring down one hip of the fitted skirt drew the eye to her slender curvaceousness. The middle-aged banker's eyes kept straying to her body, taking in everything all the way from her pumps up the slim, nyloned legs, traversing the curves of hip, waist and bust to the golden fairness of her throat. Seated beside Roan de la Corte, Analisa felt exactly like what the lecherous old fool took her to be. Sitting quietly, her hands clutching her kid handbag so tightly that her shining, unpolished nails whitened beneath the pressure, she fought the urge to explain, to cry out in denial of the man's lewd thoughts, while inwardly she cursed Roan for deliberately putting her in this position.

Yet it wasn't the dress alone that had misled the man, she knew, for she had never worn immodest clothes and therefore owned none. Rather, it was the possessive way Roan's hand had touched her back, her arm, as he had guided her through the door and made the introductions, his hand never losing contact throughout the interview with some part of her body. Only she could see the cool grey mockery behind the intimate caress of his eyes. He might as well have omitted her name altogether and said simply, "This is my mistress, Mr. Hardman," when introducing her. Roan touched her arm, his long fingers lingering on her skin, and suddenly through her haze of misery she realized, as he slipped the cashier's check carelessly into his breast pocket, that the interview was over. She had spoken not one word; she was humiliatingly aware that she had been on display, and that she had been there for no other purpose. And now she must go display herself to Antone Costenza, while Roan handed over the check that would give him the right to do with her as he pleased.

"Your first bidder?" she asked bitterly when they were alone.

"Bidder?" Bafflement drew his black brows together.

"I'm not a fool, Roan!" she snapped. "I know when I've been put on display like—like a piece of *whoremeat.*"

His hand tightened warningly over hers the instant before he handed her into the car. "You've been doing fine, Analisa. Don't spoil it." The unexpected gentleness in his voice caused her to look up in surprise, catching an expression of warmth on his unguarded face, but his eyes hardened to ice at the sight of the tears dancing like dew in a coppery spiderweb at the tips of her lashes.

"I haven't, you know," she said softly, "but I know what I owe you. I'll keep trying."

Analisa was grateful for Roan's reticence on the drive to the palatial Costenza house in Fountain Hills in the desert foothills east of the city, for had he spoken she could not have opened her mouth in reply without bursting into tears.

At the center of the massive house, which Analisa found garish and tawdry, they were met by a reception committee of five in what she guessed could only be an ill-disguised gaming room. Antone Costenza she recognized, but the three men with him were strangers whose names she was too befuddled to remember. Beside the man Roan generally referred to (with, she noticed, a degree of acerbity) as "Cousin Tone" stood a voluptuous, dark-haired, exquisitely turned-out young woman of about twenty-five. She looked vaguely familiar, and Analisa wondered at first if she might be Antone's mistress. But under the same roof as his wife? And then Roan was repeating the woman's name, Luisa Costenza, and in an instant it all came back to Analisa: the dark-haired, pale-eyed beauty who had clung to Roan's arm that night of Analisa's graduation dance, who had unwittingly provoked Analisa's childish jealousy because Roan had touched her hair. . . .

Analisa roused from her trance to realize that she herself was now the object of jealous scrutiny, and wondered how, with no less than three years for the pursuit having elapsed, Roan had eluded capture. Luisa's eyes were like bluish pinpoints of fire burning into her, and Analisa shivered, a reaction invisible to the eye yet obviously apparent to Roan who stood close beside her, for his glance swept keenly over her. Encircling her shoulder possessively with his right arm, he used his left hand to remove the cashier's check from his jacket and pass it to Antone Costenza.

"Have I your word that all Costenza family doors are closed to Orlando Avalon, and that no harm will ever come to him or to his daughter?" As he spoke, his arm tightened about Analisa's shoulder, and with calculated deliberateness his fingertips feathered her breast and lingered there. A slow, dangerous fire began to seep upward through Analisa's loins as she strived to maintain her icy aloofness.

"The Costenza doors are closed to Orlando Avalon," Antone began in a rumbling voice while his three male companions nodded in silent assent, "but beyond that, I can make guarantees only for myself and my brethren." Her attention riveted, Analisa looked at the speaker sharply, then followed his amused glance to his granddaughter, whose extraordinarily perfect face was distorted with rage. There was blood and lust in her hot eyes as they rested on Roan's hand at Analisa's breast, and Analisa knew she'd made a dangerous enemy. With the cunning of a chameleon, Luisa suddenly smiled devastatingly and stepped away from her grandfather to enclose Roan's face between her hands and kiss him full and passionately on the mouth. She withdrew her lips just enough to murmur coaxingly, "How much did you pay for her, darling, and how long will it take her to repay the loan?" Analisa seethed with the realization that Roan must have confided in this woman. She would have snatched herself from Roan's embrace, but at that moment he released her to grip both of Luisa's arms.

"Don't push your luck, Luisa," he hissed softly, savagely, against her encroaching mouth. "If by now you don't know how I feel about pushy women, you're a remarkably slow learner." He set her forcefully from him, lifted Analisa's hand mockingly to his lips, nodded curtly to the men, and led his captive from the room.

In the car, Analisa stared numbly at her escort. He touched her cheek, smiling enigmatically. "Go on, say it!" he urged. "Get it out of your system. It's your last chance, because from now on you're mine to do with, and there'll be no hedging or cheating."

Despite her resolve to remain aloof, she heard herself saying, "Perhaps my role isn't quite as I'd imagined. My function is to make Luisa Costenza jealous, isn't it? Though it hardly seems necessary. She'd marry you today if you asked her."

"She'd have married me a year ago if I'd asked her," he responded. "Three years ago. But I haven't asked her." With an air of finality he turned his attention to starting the car. As they coasted downhill toward the wide boulevard with its world-famous high-shooting fountain, he said, "I'll take you to pick up your car now so you can get to work. Remember, dinner at eight; we'll have to leave the house by half past seven. Will you have time for lunch with me now?"

He spoke with such casual friendliness that she looked at him in astonishment for a moment before shaking her head. "If I'm to be ready by seven-thirty, I'd better not. I've a lot to do at the restaurant." She had thought she would like nothing better than to be free of her captor, but to her confusion, she half-regretted her previous commitment.

Waiting at the boulevard for traffic to clear, he caught her face in one hand, his thumb and forefinger sinking painfully into her cheeks, bringing tears to her eyes. "You're much too agreeable, Analisa. What little tricks are you planning?"

"No tricks," she whispered. "I intend to make myself agreeable." She gulped hard. "For forty-seven thousand dollars, aren't you entitled to that?" When he continued to stare at her suspiciously, she wrested her head angrily out of his grasp. "Damn you, Roan, don't make me grovel! Don't humiliate me!" And then to her utter humiliation the tears spilled from her eyes and began to slip silently down her cheeks. She turned away quickly. "Just—just drive, Mr. de la Corte. I'll be all right in a minute, and it won't happen again." To prove herself she faced him again shortly, her eyes dry and hard, her voice crisp and businesslike.

"Generally I work Tempe on Tuesdays, Scottsdale on Thursdays and Phoenix on Saturdays. Will that suit your plans, or will I need to reschedule my days?"

A satisfied smile played at the corners of his mouth. "That's fine. As long as I know so that I can work around your schedule. Just keep in mind that by this time next month, you will have arranged to devote all your time to me."

"I'll have to confer with Daddy as to whom best to entrust our secrets—"

"You are *not* to go to the house. Have him meet you at the restaurant."

"It would be a good opportunity to pick up the rest of my things—"

"I've already arranged about that with your father's housekeeper. Your clothes will have been delivered by the time you get home this evening."

"Home," he'd said. She felt as if a cold wind had blown across her heart.

Returning from work, she let herself into the house with the key Roan had given her since it was not Ardith's day in. Just as he'd said, the remainder of her wardrobe had arrived and was hanging neatly in place along with all the things she'd left unpacked the previous night. Had Roan made himself so familiar, or had he arranged for her father's maid to come in? Half angrily, she selected her lingerie and hurried to the bathroom to bathe; having no idea where they were dining or with whom she left the selection of gown until she could consult with Roan.

He had still not arrived when she had finished bathing. After a moment's doubt she pulled on the negligee she had worn the previous night, having hung it near the tub to steam out the wrinkles, and crept into Roan's room to use his bedside phone. Her father had not appeared at the restaurant all afternoon, and she urgently needed to gain his approval of her choice of successor so that she could begin training without delay. Fumbling in the darkened room she switched on a lamp beside the bed, then stepped backwards violently. On Roan's nightstand was Tanny's photograph of herself, snapped in that instant of transcendent joy. Herself. Her mother. Whatever her father had seen in that picture, it had been his most treasured possession. Her hand trembled so much that she had to dial three times before she got her father's number right. Fortunately he answered promptly, but she had not yet launched into the purpose of her call when behind her Roan's authoritative voice warned, "Hang up, Analisa. You know the rules."

She gasped, whirling to face him where he was leaning on the corner of a broad cherrywood dresser, studying her speculatively. Interrupting her father's eager words she said hastily, "I'm sorry, Daddy, I have to go now. But it's imperative you come to the Scottsdale restaurant Thursday so we can agree about my successor. I'm sure Mr. de la Corte has discussed this with you. Bye now." She cut him off in mid-protest, feeling mean and small and furiously at a disadvantage.

Tears stung her eyes as she cried out in frustration, "That was Daddy's favorite picture! Did you have to take that from him, too?"

He studied her expressionlessly for fully a minute before a smile transformed his face. "It's inscribed, 'With all my love, Analisa.' It seems that it more appropriately belongs to me now."

She gasped. "But I *hate* you!" she whispered.

"Are you quite certain, Analisa?"

60

Was she? She felt her color rising, and she began to clench and unclench her fists at her sides. At least the light was behind her, obscuring the telltale color in her face. In the next instant she realized just how much of her body would conversely be revealed by that light shining through her filmy gown.

Roan's eyes narrowed and his smile vanished. "Come here, Analisa." Defiant of the quiet menace in his voice, her feet remained rooted. "If I have to come to you . . ." he warned as his eyes moved toward the bed. Before he could complete his threat she hurried to stand before him. She wanted, as she had never before wanted, to strike out at him, and she gripped her hands tightly behind her back, too agitated to realize how provocatively her small, lovely breasts thrust forward in such a stance. "One step closer," he commanded softly, and, mesmerized, she obeyed.

With smooth movements his right hand pinned her clasped hands behind her while his left glided across her cheek, her neck, her shoulder, pushing her negligee gently aside and coming to rest against her satiny skin, his index finger teasing the pulse that hammered in her throat. It was as if he'd poured liquid fire over her, engulfing her in flame. "Tell me again that you hate me," he taunted, his lips close to hers.

"I do. I do," she insisted, her mind reeling, and in the next instant he pulled her against his own hard, languid length. His lips teased hers, plucking gently at first her upper lip, then her lower one, until she found herself relaxing helplessly against the pleasurable demands of his body. He laughed with soft, provocative insolence. "Your kind of hate I can live with." As he spoke he slipped his hand beneath her bra strap, coaxing it aside, his thumb claiming one traitorously hardening nipple.

She stiffened in his embrace and willed herself to stare at him defiantly, though knowing she had forfeited her right to deny him whatever he chose to take. "It's past seven. We're going to be late. Who are these people we're meeting tonight?" She spoke with determined coolness, but a slight, amused gleam in his eyes told her he was not fooled by her feigned indifference or her delaying tactics. He lowered his head to taste briefly of her undeniable arousal before deftly replacing her bra strap and smoothing her gown over her shoulder.

"Not people. Person. Jules Goldfarb, a New York client interested in commissioning a pair of earrings yet to be designed. He won't be expecting you, so he'll be pleasantly surprised." He released her to swat her bottom playfully. "Go dress. Wear the gold Grecian thing."

So. He *had* been the one to install her wardrobe, familiarizing himself with her fashions. She walked away from him on unsteady legs, mutinously refusing to meet his eyes.

There was not a moment of the evening when Roan, seated so that his knee beneath the table remained in contact with Analisa's thigh, was not aware of his partner's tension. Her gown, floating layers of irridescent chiffon over an ivory body glove, reflected the colors of her surroundings. It laid bare one shoulder, its décolletage suggesting rather than exposing an enticing cleavage. She wore metallic gold sling-heel pumps and ivory elbow-length gloves and carried a gold mesh bag. Her darker bronze-gold hair was upswept high on her head to imbue her with an air of sophistication.

When Roan had come to inspect and approve, he had handed her a pair of ebony earrings, tear drops suspended from golden sepals, their very simplicity a mark of elegance. "Wear these," he had commanded, "as models of de la Corte craftsmanship." Before threading the posts into her ears with shaking hands, she had seen the stallion engraved at the base of one sepal and had known she was entrusted with a treasure.

Roan had helped her into her black mink jacket, his hands resting overlong on her shoulders, and at Camelback Inn where their guest waited, he'd removed it, his hands sliding possessively down the length of her arms as he did so, publicly and clearly proclaiming his proprietorship. All through dinner, his middle-aged client had scarcely taken his greedy eyes from Analisa's stunningly perfect body. At last, pushing aside his plate, Mr. Goldfarb extracted a platinum cigarette case and, opening it, proffered it to Analisa, at the same time suggesting that an after-dinner liqueur would be appreciated. Desperate for something to do with her hands now that they were no longer engaged with her dinner silver, Analisa reached for a cigarette. Though she had never smoked before, she hoped she could bluff her way through. Roan's hand was suddenly on hers. "We don't smoke," he stated with unnecessary force. "The delicacy of my work demands absolutely steady nerves, to which nicotine is not conducive, and the secondhand smoke of such a constant companion as Analisa would be as damaging as if I smoked myself." Analisa's teeth clenched at the implication of intimacy which she was powerless to contradict. His hand tightened warningly on her wrist as he added, "For the same reason, I restrict myself to one drink an evening. However, by all means, feel free to order whatever you wish, both of you." With a graceful flick of his wrist he summoned a waiter and placed their order; an angel's wing for Analisa, and for his client an apricot brandy and curaçao, with lime.

Jules Goldfarb leaned back in his chair and squinted at Analisa through the stratus of his smoke. "Something similar to your model's earrings would be appropriate for my wife, I think," he announced suddenly, coming at last to the purpose of the evening's entertainment. He sat forward suddenly, ostensibly to touch the pendants at her lobes, but in fact his pudgy hands began to stroke her ears and neck. Analisa stiffened suddenly, sloshing her drink onto the snowy cloth, and Roan felt her fury like a jolt through his knee where it rested against her leg. Quickly she withdrew her hands from her glass to grip them in her lap, her chin lifting ever so slightly in an effort to dislodge the prowling hands without causing an unpleasant scene. Beneath the table Roan placed a warm, warning and yet somehow oddly comforting hand over Analisa's.

"What suits Analisa would not necessarily suit Mrs. Goldfarb," he said, and there was no mistaking the authority in his voice. "Her coloring, the shape of her face . . . It's unfortunate your wife didn't accompany you. Perhaps you have a photo of her in your wallet?" Thus diverted, the man removed his hands, and when Roan had studied the offered picture, he asked. "How tall is your wife, Mr. Goldfarb?"

"Oh," the man pondered, leaning forward to touch Analisa again, "I should think about as tall as your . . . *companion* here,"—a note of self-righteous contempt there —"though not as slim." Before he could touch her again, Analisa rose abruptly.

"If you will excuse me, Mr. de la Corte, I'll freshen up while you gentlemen discuss your business."

As she glided away, trying not to bolt from the table, she heard Roan saying contemplatively, "The pendant design would suit your wife, but with her dark coloring, I would suggest gold drops hung from ruby sepals. . . ."

Several minutes later, her composure almost secure, Analisa returned, threading her way toward the two men. Roan had tilted his chair back, hands in his trouser pockets, and was saying, "Jewels are merely invaluable; today, the only truly priceless gem is a virgin." He heard Analisa's gasp behind him, and turned to smile enigmatically at her, rising and taking her hand as he seated her. Her face was a blank white mask. What—or who—was he really here to sell? She felt like naked flesh being paraded on an auction block. "Would you believe," Roan said conversationally, continuing to address his client, "I once paid forty-seven thousand dollars for such a treasure?" He felt the trembling of her hand, noted Analisa's paleness and the incredulous shimmer of tears in her sea-green eyes, and instead of releasing her, he lifted her again to her feet, announcing, "But enough of business, Mr. Goldfarb. Will you excuse us for one dance?"

On the crowded dance floor Roan's arm tightened about her as he murmured, "Keep smiling at all costs, my dear. In customer relations, you do not offend the customer. Our client is watching you hungrily, a starved wolf, and any second now he's going to cut in. And you, my dear, are going to be *very* cooperative with him." She had been gliding smoothly

with him, as attuned to his step as if she were a part
of him; now she brought her spike heel down
vehemently against his instep. In the same instant,
as predicted, Jules Goldfarb claimed her. "She's all
yours!" Roan abruptly relinquished her and went off
to dance with one girl after another who throughout
dinner had been ogling him with this obvious
purpose—among others—in their minds.

Without respite, Mr. Goldfarb clamped Analisa
tightly against his corpulent body, pulling her off
balance, and as his excitement mounted his perspi-
ration became offensive. She submitted, though
unresponsively, to his verbal endearments, but
when he leaned forward to nibble her ear she backed
off so violently she missed half a dozen steps. Jerking
her head away, her blazing eyes encountered Roan's
as he danced nearby with a ravishing auburn-haired
girl. Analisa's partner seemed, if anything, more excited by her resistance, and his thick lips again
sought her ear. To her astonishment, anger hardened Roan's features, and a moment later he steered
his partner close. "Should we change partners,
Jules? I know how sensitive you are to beauty, and it
seems a shame for me to monopolize it. Joy, this is
Jules Goldfarb, a visiting dignitary from New York.
Analisa, shall we?"

"If you wish, Mr. de la Corte," she murmured icily.
Before either of their partners quite knew what had
happened, Roan had claimed her and in a series of
graceful turns brought them to their table. There, instead of seating her, he tore a sheet off a small note
pad on which Analisa recognized a design for earrings similar to those she was modeling. Folding the
paper, he placed it in his breast pocket.

"As soon as our client finishes this dance, we'll say

good-night." Occupied with the task of placing several large-denomination bills on the check tray, Roan didn't see the fascination with which Analisa watched the throbbing at his temple. He was furiously angry, and she could only hope it was with Jules Goldfarb for the liberties he had taken.

But once settled in his luxurious Mercedes, Roan turned on her to say with barely controlled rage, "Don't *ever* try that again, Analisa."

It was fully a minute before she could contain her own anger enough to respond. "Your client was being obnoxious—at, I might say, practically your invitation—and you blame *me*. . . ."

His hand came up swiftly and captured her chin ungently. "No games, Analisa. You know what I'm talking about. Had you not chosen to defy me in such a physical manner, I'd not have abandoned you to Goldfarb. I know a greasy pig when I see one. You got what you deserved."

She tried to speak, but her mouth trembled, tears burned on her sweeping lashes, and she knew she could not utter a word without disgracing herself. With all her physical and emotional strength she tried to get a grip on herself.

"And another thing." His voice grew strangely gentle. "The name is Roan. Mistresses don't generally go around addressing their lovers as *Mr.*"

She lifted her chin. "Am I to be your mistress then, *Roan*? I thought perhaps you meant to . . . s-sell me—"

"I've paid a dear dollar for you, Analisa. You will be mine first."

"Indeed, Mr. de la Corte," she responded coolly. "And when did you arrive at that decision?"

"Roan," he corrected firmly, adding fiercely,

"When I saw you in Goldfarb's arms. No man has the right to hold you that way, and until I tell you otherwise I'd better never find you so much as looking at another man."

"How then," she demanded recklessly, "do you propose to sell me to the highest bidder?"

"Shut up!" His hands gripped her arms, and he shook her furiously. For one insane instant she imagined she had seen anguish in his eyes, but the bitterness of his next words brought her to her senses. "Do you think I'm likely to find a bidder who will pay more for you than I already have? You're mine, and mine you will remain until I'm ready to share you."

CHAPTER 5

DESPITE the urgency of the matter, Analisa's father did not put in an appearance at the Scottsdale restaurant until midafternoon Thursday. By that time Analisa was dusted from head to toe with flour, and was not at a satisfactory stopping point. As Orlando came in the back door, she noticed an uncharacteristic shuffle to his gait, and her heart ached at his hangdog attitude. His face was flushed, his brown eyes avoided hers, his pants were wrinkled and his expensive blue sports shirt showed careless spillage down the front. Shocked at such a transformation in just three days, she said gently, "I'll be through here in another hour, Daddy. Why don't you go into the bar and wait for me?" She immediately regretted her suggestion, for when he paused to kiss her, there was no doubt what had caused the dramatic decline in his appearance. "On second thought," she amended desperately, forcing a laugh to conceal her dismay, "why not help me and I can be done in half the time?"

He grinned sheepishly. "Twice the time, you mean," he quipped with a slight slurring of his words. "I'll take your original advice."

When Analisa was at last able to leave the kitchen, she saw her father morosely alone at one end of the half-empty crescent-moon bar. Unobserved, she watched him quaff an ale in almost a single gulp and signal the bartender with raised stein for another. Hastening across the room, she caught Bill Dunstan's eye and shook her head vehemently. Trapped between the boss's daughter, who had right on her side, and the boss, who had the might, the bartender looked at if he would like to evaporate. Reaching her father's side, Analisa smiled sympathetically at the man, who was nervously switching the empty stein from hand to hand, and explained, "We have to be on our way, but thanks, Bill."

Her father pulled at her hand, dragging her down onto a vacant stool, and too late she realized the last hour's drinking had made him maudlin and vociferous. In a loud voice, the slurring of his words now sickeningly pronounced, he demanded, "Hazh he made you go to bed with him yet, little one?" Tears began to stream down his face, and suddenly the entire lounge quieted, listening entranced. "Jus' gimme the word an' I'll kill him for you."

Every eye in the room was upon them, and as Analisa fought to retain her dignity she was grateful that only a few customers were there to witness her shame and embarrassment. "I'll take you home, Daddy," she said softly but forcefully. "You're in no condition to drive." She helped him to his feet, stumbling under his weight as he meekly obeyed. As the swinging saloon half-doors closed behind them a low babble of voices erupted in their wake, and Analisa wished for herself the impossible luxury of her father's uninhibited tears.

He relinquished the keys to his silver-bullet Buick without resistance, but the moment they were seated together in the car his humility was supplanted by hostility. "Well, has he?" he shouted.

Let him think her crimson face the result of anger. As resolutely as she could, she reminded him, "I told you how it is with Roan and me, Daddy, and you'll have to accept that I . . . I've chosen to live with him of my own free will. My sex life is not something I ever have or ever will discuss with you—or anyone." How much she wanted to tell him the truth, but how impossible that was now.

"You filthy tramp!" he roared, raising his hand as if to strike her.

"Don't, Daddy," she warned him dispassionately. "You hate yourself enough without adding to your burden." He collapsed against the door with a sob, and they drove in tormented silence the few miles to his Camelback home. Helping him to his den, she was distressed to see the state of his built-in bar— several bottles half-empty, dirty glasses overturned on a tray as if he had been drinking steadily ever since she had left on Monday. She wondered how he had ever driven himself to the restaurant, and then, angrily, what the housekeeper could have been thinking to let him drive in his inebriated condition, or to let his study and his person get into such a disgraceful state. Suddenly it occurred to her that Gladys Fenster, by choice or by dismissal, might no longer be employed here. "I'll make you some coffee," she said gently. "Just rest here on the couch."

The coffee set to brew, she was about to go in search of the housekeeper when Gladys huffed in through the rear entrance, slapping a large sack of groceries onto the counter. Before she could speak,

Analisa was arrested by the woman's outraged glare. "So I hope you're happy with yourself, Miss! Did you publish it in the Republic? Not bedded two nights with your lover and it all comes back to your poor father his first visit to his own club where he once was a man of stature. All of them jaws yakking and the snide remarks, and you with no regard or care for him as raised you to be decent and fine. I thank God every day your lovely mother is gone from us and beyond shame."

Analisa stood transfixed throughout this diatribe, her face blanched, her fists curled at her sides. "I'm glad he has one loyal friend," she managed to say at last over the racking pain in her chest. "I was just fixing him some coffee, which he badly needs. Will you bring it to him in his study when it's ready, Gladys? And I'd appreciate it if you would clean up the mess in there, and see to it that in the future he doesn't have so much opiate at his disposal."

The broad-faced woman snorted. "And how do you plan I should do that, Miss, when he holds the purse? If you didn't have hormones where your brains ought to be—" Analisa, unable to bear the housekeeper's vindictiveness any longer, bolted through the door.

Orlando Avalon lay sprawled untidily on the beige leather couch. Analisa stared down at him. "Daddy, I have to talk to you, and I only have this one time to say it all. You recall that years ago you entrusted our pastry recipes to Jeanette and our sauces to Juan in Tucson. When you sold those restaurants, you left them without work. Today I heard that Jeanette and Juan are getting married—and that they are talking about opening a restaurant of their own using *our* recipes. Are you with me, Daddy?"

He was lying with eyes closed, a resigned look on his puffy face. "Sure, little one, sure. You think I'm drunk just because I'm feeling good—"

"You're feeling rotten, Daddy, and you know it," Analisa contradicted without rancor. "I have to turn over my work—and that means our family secrets—to someone else within the month. I'm sure Roan has already discussed this with you. I wanted to talk to you about it, also, but since you haven't given me an opportunity and there won't be another, I'm going to have to use my own judgment. I'm going to ask Jeanette and Juan to come back to work for us. They'll be expensive, you can be sure—probably exorbitant, since they're in a position to call the shots and they know it. Do you understand me?"

"Sure, little one, sure," he said bitterly. "I understand you're selling me short—"

"Oh, Daddy," she wailed, "I love you! Please don't let this destroy you—destroy us. We just have to hold our heads up and show the world—"

"—Show the world that you've turned me out! That's what de la Corte wanted. You fool! Once he gets you pregnant how long do you think it'll be before he goes running back to Luisa Costenza or one of his other feisty little fillies—"

The door swung open behind Analisa with a whoosh. Embarrassed by her father's tirade she asked over her shoulder, "Is the coffee ready, Gladys?" The only response was slow, measured breathing, and some pulsating force quivering angrily in the air impelled her to whirl about.

Roan stood there very still, condemnation in his cold grey eyes and an uncompromising set to his jaw. She stared at him, lips half-parted in protest while her eyes begged his forbearance. After a long moment of tacit entreaty, she spoke swiftly to her father. "Unless you contact me at work during my regular hours, I'll have to use my own judgment, Daddy. I'm sorry you feel I've betrayed you. I do love you. Nothing can change that. I've asked Gladys to bring you some black coffee."

He lurched to a sitting position. "Get out, you whore!" he snarled thickly. With a muffled cry she spun from him, only to encounter Roan's eyes, nearly colorless with rage. She lifted her chin proudly, refusing to satisfy him with a show of her pain, and marched square-shouldered through the door he opened for her. As the beige leather door swung closed behind them, she heard her father's long sob, and in spite of herself she caught Roan's hand and clung to it. Not a word was spoken between them as he showed her to his car.

As they drove back to the restaurant in silence, Analisa's thoughts and emotions were in total confusion. It hadn't occurred to her that Roan would check up on her, but even if it had, she still would have driven her father home. Let Roan argue that she could have delegated the job to someone else; the fact remained that she'd had to speak to her father about her replacement. Besides, her father was her responsibility, no one else's. She knew she had assured Roan, when he'd given his check to Antone Costenza, that she meant to be obedient and agreeable—but how could she be when he was so unreasonable and unfeeling! And worse still, as her father had known all along, Roan meant to take from her the one thing that she could give but once, and then, having gratified his lust, he would flaunt his other women in her face. And then he would sell her to the next bidder, and the next, and the next. The prospect horrified her, but it inexplicably wounded her as well. She had seen the way feminine eyes turned toward Roan whenever he entered a room, the way women offered themselves shamelessly. His successes with women were almost as well known as his success in art and business.

But why should his callousness hurt her? What did his hard heart mean to her? She detested Roan de la Corte! He had ruined her life. Her litany of hate paraded through her mind until she closed her eyes tightly against the pain of it. Even so, she was instantly aware of the moment they drew into the parking lot beside her car, and, straightening, she reached for the door handle to let herself out and flee, if only for a few minutes, Roan's tormenting presence. He switched off the ignition and turned toward her, a signal that she was to remain where she was. She faced him rebelliously and was disconcerted to see only genuine concern in his softened features.

"You've got enough on your plate already, Analisa," he said gently. "I only wish you wouldn't force me to spell it out for you." His eyes had turned silvery sad, and she held her breath waiting for him to continue. "The Costenza family doesn't control all the gaming in Arizona. My cousin Antone can protect you from his own family, but there are rivals over whom he has no control. Rivals who might, in fact, welcome an opportunity to avenge old scores. You are not safe from them, Analisa, and neither is your father." The stillness of his hands where they rested on the steering wheel seemed to emphasize the deadly validity of his words, and her eyes grew large with fear. "I'm sorry, Analisa. I really don't want to frighten you, but if he gets into trouble again, you'll be no better off than you were before you came to me. I'm not a Hunt or a Rockefeller or an Onassis, that I can go on indefinitely bailing your father out."

She licked her lips and tried to speak, but no sounds came. After a while, he continued, "Though he's not going to admit it, your father knows as well as you and I do that he's never going to quit gambling. Still, he's no more anxious than I am to see you used as live bait, and at least he's doing a commendable job of convincing the world that you and he no longer claim kinship. Short of quitting his habit, that's the only kindness he can do you.

"As a matter of fact, Analisa, he has already started gambling with so-called friends at his club in an effort to win enough money to buy you back from me, though I made it perfectly clear to him at the outset that there was absolutely no repurchase option. He has been drinking too much, and talking too much, and by now I imagine the redoubtable Gladys Fenster has carried the banner proclaiming your promiscuity into such public places as the supermarket, the spa, and her bridge club. She has no doubt even succeeded in convincing your father of your culpability which, however much it hurts, is all to the good. Only when he bitterly and publicly denounces you and convinces the enemy of his sincerity will you be truly safe. As for Gladys, don't be hurt by her betrayal. She once worked for my mother, who had to dismiss her because of her vindictiveness. She was never your friend; the loss of her is nothing."

The tears she'd been holding at bay slid silently down her cheeks. When she could control her voice, she confessed softly, "Roan, a minute ago I was hating you."

He smiled with a sad warmth that touched her heart. "I know."

"I'm sorry. Just when I think you're the devil incarnate you invariably turn out to be quite the opposite." She pushed down the door handle, and as the door swung open beneath her touch, she asked, "Will I see you at your house in a few minutes?"

"At *our* house, yes," he replied, smiling. "I'm right behind you all the way."

She twisted in the seat and dropped her feet to the ground, then turned to ask, "Have you any plans for this evening? May I fix you dinner at home tonight?"

"*Dîner à deux* and early bed," he concurred, and then smiled somewhat satanically at the alarm that surfaced briefly in her eyes.

"You're sure you wouldn't like to go out?" Roan asked as Analisa began clearing up the dishes from the kitchen bar where they'd dined informally. She had prepared a Mexican-style supper, a simple torte of ground beef, cheese and corn tortillas, and mashed potatoes baked with golden cream corn and cheddar cheese, spiced lightly with chopped jalapeños. She thought he'd shown more enthusiasm for her simple menu than he had on the previous two evenings when they'd dined out in lavish style.

She shook her head wearily. "Two consecutive nights and a tough day at work are rather my limit, I think."

He smiled impudently. "You sound like an old married woman."

"I thought it was old married men who refused to budge from the comfort of their armchairs at night," she countered, "while their housebound wives retaliated by compiling lists of grievances for the lawyer.

What I'd really like to do is curl up in front of a roaring fire with a good book and some soft music."

"Close," he concurred, carrying his own dishes to the sink. "Close," and when she looked askance, he clarified, "I'd prefer to curl up with soft music and a good woman."

She stood immobile, staring at him, soft lovely color trespassing across her chin to her cheeks. He watched the agitated rise and swell of her breasts as she struggled for composure before letting his gaze sweep up to her face. "You have very expressive eyes," he murmured, feathering the tips of his fingers along her jawline.

"And what do they say to you?" she asked fearfully.

He kissed her softly on the lips, a downy touch that made her heart kick over once with fervor. Huskily he answered, "They tell me you're frightened. They tell me you're not ready yet. Contrary to what your heart tells me," he teased as his hand cupped her left breast and set her heart racing. "Your body wants to become a woman's body, Analisa. Why have you bound your mind with chains?"

"I haven't, Roan. For my own protection, my loving parents did. Because they cared, I was taught by word and act to believe in the sanctity of love, marriage and family. It never for an instant occurred to me that—" her pain-filled gaze slid away from his, and she stared at some invisible, vanquished dream beyond his shoulder—"that these things were to be denied me. I promise you, Roan, I'm trying to . . . to cooperate, but it isn't easy to turn one's back on a lifetime's discipline." She withdrew from his light embrace, ashamed of the tears that never seemed far away, and turning her back on him she busied herself with arranging the dirty dishes and running detergent and water into the dishwasher.

As she bent to her task, his hand swept aside the long fall of her deep gold hair, and he dropped a light kiss on the nape of her neck. "The lady wishes a fire, and a fire she shall have. Make us a fresh pot of coffee, okay?"

When she appeared in the library a few minutes later with the silver coffee pot and stoneware mugs on a lacquered tray, a welcoming fire blazed in the great native stone and turquoise fireplace, and Beethoven's *Fugue in A Minor* issued softly from hidden speakers placed strategically about the room. "Does the music suit, or would you prefer something less sedate?" Roan was kneeling on a luxurious rust-colored angora rug before the hearth, tending the fire. He looked up at her with caressing eyes that did unexpected, disquieting things to her nerves.

"It's lovely. The whole room is lovely. I've never been in here before." Placing the tray on a fruitwood coffee table with shaking hands, she looked about appreciatively at the paloverde paneling, the carpeting of mottled browns, the drapes of terra-cotta and gold. The couch, chairs and hassocks were all upholstered in beige, browns and rusts, and in one corner, where her father would have placed a liquor cabinet, stood a no-nonsense desk. The earth tones gave the room the serene quality of a retreat. She moved to touch one of the random turquoise-colored stones of the fireplace. "Is it really turquoise?" she asked wonderingly. "I do believe one could just about build an entire house on the proceeds from this one fireplace."

"Some of it is turquoise, while the richer blue is azurite. Both are inferior by-products of the Bisbee and Morenci copper mines."

Nodding, she turned her attention to the examination of colorful, highly polished stones casually arranged on the mantelpiece—nuggets of Brazilian amethyst, tubular rock crystals on a bed of sparkling, diamondlike drusy quartz. There was a twisted chunk of coral from Italy looking not unlike a weathered cedar tree trunk, as well as the brilliant kinds of deposits one finds in the western mining areas: cinnabar as bright as new blood, a slab of green malachite pearls, the paislied navies and greens of anglesite/galena and an almost defiant blend of blue azurite combined with green malachite—beautiful specimens that needed no special lighting to reveal their brilliance. "A man's kind of jewelry," she pronounced. "Too beautiful to be broken down into the fine stuff women wear." She knelt before a barite stone which stood alone beside the hearth and touched a single small desert rose in a larger chunk of petallike clusters the color of the Mojave desert at sunset. "Now this," she suggested, caressing the unfinished roughness of the stone, "would make a gorgeous ring, and here are two slightly larger roses for matching earrings."

Roan laughed with languid pleasure. "Too soft for jewelry, my love," and at the endearment her fingers stumbled in their exploration. "At the first slight blow, they'd break like a woman's heart." She turned slightly to give him a startled, inquiring look, searching for the cynicism she'd expected to find in his face. She hadn't realized how close they were.

"Do you do your own rock-hounding on location, or

do you plunder the local rock shops for your treasures?" she asked quickly to hide her nervousness.

"A bit of both. I prefer doing my own, when time permits, though with the do-it-yourself mania of the past dozen years a find is truly a treasure. Are you a rock hound?"

"Sometimes," she said sadly, "before money got in the way of living, we used to go out camping, and we could never resist looking. But there's so little resemblance between the rock in the ground and the polished product, I suppose we never really knew what we were looking for—or at. But we didn't care. Our pleasure was in our togetherness. The real treasure was in the seeking, not the finding. In time, though, there were more and more restaurants, operating for more and more hours, and gradually there was less and less time for family life. By the time I was seventeen, our outings had long since become a thing of the past." She lowered her head disconsolately, and her rich gold lashes made crescent shadows on her lovely high cheekbones. She sighed deeply, and said with a Mona Lisa smile, "We were so much richer when we were poor."

Roan was watching her with such disconcerting compassion that she rose unsteadily to her feet, knowing that in this moment she was far too susceptible to his dangerous charisma. She crossed the room to study the floor-to-ceiling bookshelves that covered one entire wall. Her finger, running along the backs of the books, came to a sudden halt. "These are your mother's books," she said almost accusingly.

"Some of them are," he said agreeably, coming to stand behind her. "Which ones in particular?" She was startled by the closeness of his voice and glanced uneasily over her shoulder to see that he was almost touching her.

"All of these," she replied, removing herself by one step and sweeping her hand over a section which held treatises on child psychology and books about the emotionally disturbed child.

"And how did you deduce that they are my mother's?" Roan asked quizzically.

"The one thing Paris de la Corte and I have in common is the school for disturbed children, though our paths seldom cross since she, of course, is an administrative volunteer, while I work directly with the children."

"What a remarkable avocation for one so young," he marveled.

She studied him at length before answering, trying to detect any unkind criticism in either his voice or expression. "Yes, so a great many people seem to think. I took my mother's place when she was—when she died. At the time, it seemed merely the proper thing to do, considering the desperate need for volunteers, but now I wouldn't give it up for anything. It's exhausting, frustrating, and sometimes downright hazardous—for disturbed children are not infrequently violent children—but it's infinitely rewarding to hear a ten-year-old boy speak his first words, or see a nine-year-old girl graduate at last from diapers." Her gaze slid away, but not before he glimpsed the wretchedness in her sea-green eyes. "It's almost as if subconsciously I've always known there would be no family for me, and that I had better do what I can for other people's children." She was speaking almost to herself.

His hands caught her firmly by the shoulders.

"Why do you say you'll never have a family?" he demanded.

The challenge in the tilt of her head when she looked at him could not hide the grief in her eyes. "One man for life—to me it's the only dream worthwhile. It's never crossed my mind to think otherwise. When you have f-finished with me. . ." she shrugged, then brought her trembling mouth under firm control, "there won't be another."

His features darkened ominously, and he gripped her shoulders so tightly she winced, but made no protest. Then, with sudden gentleness, he cradled her chin between his thumb and forefinger and turned her face one way and then the other, studying her intently as if he wanted to will himself inside her skin and know her every thought, experience her every feeling. Her heart was pounding furiously as if it would willfully destroy itself on the rocks of her despair—and desire. The hot blood racing to her loins was an insult to her common sense. How could she? How *could* she feel desire for a man who would use her so shabbily? The blood that had drained from her face, leaving her white as a midnight moon, simply had to go some place, she told herself.

"You could have my baby, Analisa," he said thoughtfully, the softness of his voice turning her to butter.

Her heart rolled over once before exploding in a shower of fragmented dreams. Doubtless Roan would make beautiful, talented babies, and Analisa was acutely aware that when he touched her, even looked at her, he could send her nerves dancing along the dizzying corridors of both heaven and hell. With her natural nurturing instincts, she would have loved to have a baby—*his* baby—but in nine months when her nameless baby was born, where would Roan be? Whose kisses would delight him, whose arms would hold him at night, whose body would bring him fulfillment? "No, Roan," she said at last, her voice soft, "I don't want your baby."

There was a fleeting look of something like pain on his face, and then he was in complete control again. Silly of her to think he could care. It must have been her imagination. "Read a book," he commanded harshly, pushing her roughly from him. "I have work to do." He strode to his desk, and she selected Linda Stewart's *Same Time, Next Year*—something frivolous, since she knew she would not be able to absorb more than the lightest of froth.

Analisa sat on the couch with her legs curled beneath her, staring at the open book, not even bothering to turn the pages. At his desk Roan worked industriously for a while with his pad and colored sketch pens. When at last he looked over at the unhappy girl on the couch, she was too lost in thought to notice. Her jeans were molded around her hips and legs, and her long-sleeved western shirt was discreetly buttoned at a point between her breasts, tantalizing in what it didn't reveal. Tucked neatly into her jeans, the fine grey cotton shirt stretched taut over her rounded breasts, which ached now with a need she couldn't—or wouldn't—define.

A tear splashed onto the page, and she scrubbed at it hastily with her forefinger. "Why are you crying, Analisa?" Roan seated himself carefully beside her.

"I'm s-sorry," she stammered. "I didn't even know I was." Another tear fell, and she apologized again. "I'm afraid I've ruined your book."

He removed the unread book from her hands and laid it on the cocktail table, next to their forgotten coffee service. "What you're ruining is my nervous system," he admonished gently, straightening out the clenched fingers of her right hand. "Now, what's troubling you?"

She looked at him with helpless, pleading eyes. "He called me a whore," she confessed softly. "Daddy thinks I'm a *whore.*"

A nerve twitched in Roan's lower jaw and traveled to his temple. "Darling, having sex with one man doesn't make you a whore." Cupping her chin with one hand, his other gentle at her waist, he kissed her without passion on her soft mouth, almost as he might comfort a child.

She was instantly dismayed by the shafts of fire his lips sent spearing through her. She pulled away in confusion. "But I haven't even had that," she protested.

His hand tightened on her waist. "You will," he promised, and the pressure of his lips hardened, seeking, demanding, willing her to respond. Rising to his feet he scooped her up roughly into his arms and carried her to the deeply soft rust-colored rug in front of the fire, where he gently laid her down. She lay on her back staring up at him, eyes enormously green, wondering what to do with her awkward arms and legs. Then he stretched along the length of her body, lying on his side, propped up on one elbow, staring hypnotically into her eyes. As his thigh touched hers, flames leaped into the pit of her stomach. He brushed a tendril of gold from her forehead, then traced one finger down her throat. "I should have sent you to change into a gown and negligee before coming in here."

At his words, the fire in her loins curled so sharply that she pulled her heels up, knees elevated as if she would draw defensively into a fetal position. She smiled wryly. "Somehow I get the impression I'm already more seductive than I meant to be."

"Oh, quite," he concurred, delivering light kisses to her forehead, temples, nose, chin. "It doesn't take filmy clothes to make you seductive. Even those rape-proof pants can't conceal your desirability. Actually, I wasn't thinking of seductiveness. I was thinking of—accessibility." The timbrous quality of his voice dizzied her, and a quiver of anticipation shook her body. Suddenly he rose above her, his chest hard against her breast, and pinned her hands beside her head. His head dipped slowly until his lips found hers, gently tantalizing at first, then growing hungry as his tongue forced her mouth open, tasting, teasing, mutually delighting. With a soft moan he released her wrists to wind his hands into her golden hair and draw her head closer still. Incapable of resisting, she wound her arms tightly about his shoulders as if afraid he might escape.

His hand trailed down her throat, lingering a moment on the whiteness between the V'd lapels of her shirt, and her body arched toward him in helpless invitation. She felt the top button released, and then another—and suddenly she awakened from her spell, her body straightening rigidly.

"You're mine, Analisa," he growled against her lips. "Bought and paid for. Don't fight me."

For a moment her arms tightened about him. Still desperately wanting him, she turned her face away, her hands resting passively beside her head where minutes ago he had pinioned them with a mastery that had sent electricity crackling through every fiber of her being. They could exploit to the fullest that feral attraction that undeniably bound them together, but what would happen to her when the flames had burned to ashes? Orlando Avalon's words echoed in Analisa's mind. "Once he gets you pregnant, how long do you think it'll be before he goes running back to Luisa Costenza?"

Roan lifted his head, his silver eyes probing hers. "Have sex with me, Roan, but please don't pretend it's love." Her voice was emotionless, burying all her anguish deep inside.

"I never said it was." His eyes grew cold and hard. He smiled tightly, then slowly began to pull off her shirt. With deliberate force he broke one strap of her bra and tugged the lacy cup downward to expose her feminine loveliness. Cupping her breast possessively in one hand, he took the hard, eager nipple gently between his teeth and began to tease it with the moist tip of his tongue. She gasped with uncontrollable delight before she was able to will her body to stiffen. To take pleasure in his body would be to fall in love with him, to grow to need him, and that could only bring disaster. She lay limp and unresponsive, though it took more will than she thought she possessed.

Roan sat up, his eyes raking her with fury, but before he could speak she said quietly, "What you bought was my body, not my—my—"

"Your love?" he snarled. "What I *paid for* was a *live* body. And there are enough of those around that I don't need an automaton." He got to his feet and towered above her, his handsome face dark with disgust. She lay helplessly, accepting his contempt, pinned to the floor as surely as if he'd driven stakes through her limbs. Abruptly he turned on his heel. "I'm going out for some air."

When she was alone she sat up painfully, tucking

herself back as best she could into her torn bra and
buttoning her shirt with nerveless fingers. She stood
up weakly, then doubled with the pain of rejection.
After a moment she crossed to the desk where he had
busied himself while she had pretended to read. On
the pad was sketched an elegant black inch-wide
bracelet, filigreed with the sharp, unmistakable
stems and thick leaves of desert succulents, and set
with a single Mojave-colored desert rose. He had
cared enough to listen, and had designed a piece of
jewelry to please her. The pain doubled her again,
and she moaned softly. What a fool she was to think
she could spare herself the agony of unrequited love
by resisting his advances. She was already in love
with Roan de la Corte! She had loved him for years.
And all she'd done was humiliate him.

She made her way slowly to her room. As she
stepped into the chilly darkness, relieved only by the
dim patio lights beyond the arcadia door, she heard a
splash and realized the cold draft she felt was coming
from Roan's open patio door. She went through his
room to stand on the lighted deck and watch him
swim several lengths of the icy pool with swift, angry
strokes. So this was how he alleviated his need. But
what was she to do about her own? She stood with
her hands stuffed disconsolately into her jeans
pockets, looking lost and lonely. At last he swam to
the near edge of the pool, acknowledging her for the
first time. "Well?" His voice was bitter.

"I—I'm sorry, Roan," she stammered in a small
voice. "I promise to do better if you s-still want me."

He laughed harshly and pulled himself up out of
the pool to stand streaming and naked before her.
She stared at him in shocked, hungry, unashamed
fascination until his cruel words snapped her to at-

tention. "It so happens I don't want you, Analisa, and when you want me, you'll have to beg. And you *will* beg!"

For a moment she stood staring at him, tears of pain and shame filling her eyes. Then she whirled and sped to the security of her dark room. "Spare me your tears, Analisa," he mocked as she fled. "They're like leeches sucking at my soul."

CHAPTER 6

ANALISA heard Roan's first morning stirrings before she slept. When she woke, the sun was well up over the rock buttes behind the house, warning her that she had not been forgiven, for Roan had made a point of gently waking her each morning. Bolting from the bed and scooping up a filmy blue negligee as she went, she was still pulling it over her nightgown as she raced down the three broad steps and burst into the kitchen. Roan sat at the counter casually buttering a piece of toast, not deigning to look up. "Why didn't you wake me?" she cried accusingly. "I could have fixed your breakfast."

"Breakfast," he said scathingly, "is not what I paid for. Sit down, Analisa. Pour yourself a cup of coffee. We have to talk."

She sat gripping the edge of the counter to still the trembling of her fingers. "About what?"

"Your day's instructions." He swiveled to examine her slight figure. Her negligee, tied only at the neck, had fallen open from throat to hem revealing her flimsy nylon nightgown and the contours beneath. "I told you last night," he said, "that you don't have to wear seductive clothing to—sell your-self."

She glanced down at herself. Bright color stained her cheeks as she clutched at her negligee, sealing the gap. She had lain awake for hours, finally deciding as dawn came that her life could be bearable only if she strove to please her captor and avert his wrath. But nothing she did seemed right. Though she had vowed to be agreeable, already the morning had gone all wrong.

Roan reached out to flick away a tear, his touch endearing until his words chilled her heart. "I also told you, no more self-pitying tears. They don't impress me."

She huddled miserably on her stool, arms clamped across her stomach. "What are your instructions for the day?" she asked coolly, striving to match his aloofness. "I had intended to go to the school this morning."

"Then you'll have to change your plans. This morning you have a photographic session in my office, then lunch with me. After that, you're free. I don't recall seeing a strapless gown in your closet."

She blinked at the sudden change of topic. "I don't own one."

"Then wear a strapless bra. You do have those, I know."

She gasped, furious. "I am *not* posing in my underwear!"

"It wouldn't matter if you wore nothing at all," he snapped. "The finished picture is to be a vignette of head and shoulders. No background, no clothing to distract from the jewels you'll wear, just your head and shoulders with that flawless, preciously defended skin to complement the beauty of the jewels."

"Well, I am *not* posing in front of any photographer, male or female, in my lingerie!"

He brought his face close to hers, his grey eyes glinting with determination. "You'll pose *nude* if I tell you to."

Her jaw tightened, and for a moment she looked him straight in the eye, rage burning in her green eyes. Then, once again remembering her vow of the sleepless night before, she lowered her head. Under control again, she suggested quietly, "I have a strapless bathing suit. Will that do?"

"A bikini is fine."

"Not a bikini. A maillot. I don't have a bikini."

"My, you are old-fashioned!" he taunted her.

"I'm sorry that having paid so dearly you don't like what you got!" she snarled. Regaining her composure, she added, "If you wish, I could go buy one. I've never worn a bikini because I never believed in advertising something that isn't—wasn't—" a bare whisper, "for sale."

She almost thought she saw a gleam of compassion in his grey eyes, but if she did it was quickly subdued. "Wear what you have," he said resignedly. "There isn't time for shopping. I expect you in my office and changed before the photographer arrives at ten." With that, he left. She sat wondering how he could possibly want her to model today. She hadn't yet looked in a mirror, but she knew her face must look as ghastly as she felt. Oh, well, her lord and master beckoned. With angry resignation, she went to her room to prepare herself for the ordeal.

Arriving unannounced, she stood in the open doorway between Roan's immaculate administrative office and his disarranged studio, watching, fascinated, as he worked with miniature tools on a fine strip of gold, his left hand seemingly as skilled as the right. "You're ambidextrous!" she exclaimed admiringly, and for the first time, he noticed her presence.

"A prerequisite of the job. Though I do favor my right hand." Then seeming to recall who—or what—she was, he added coldly, "Come in and close the door. You can change in here, but you'll have to hurry—unless you want to strip before the photographer." He stood and closed the door behind her.

"In here?" She looked wildly about the room for a private corner.

"Analisa!" His voice cracked like a whip, startling her. He came and stood before her, examining her critically. "You look like you didn't get any sleep last night!" he snapped.

"I didn't!" she snapped back. "I heard you getting up before I went to sleep—"

"Lying awake all night to guard against a rape attack?" he snarled.

"Oh, Roan!" she wailed, but he cut her short.

"Don't!" If she hadn't known better, she might have thought there was entreaty in his voice before he concluded bitterly, "Don't beg. I can't stand a beggar!"

She stared at him in bewilderment. "You said last night—"

He smiled cruelly. "I said you would beg. I didn't say it would gain you anything." Analisa blanched and was speechless, the only color in her face the deep green misery of her eyes. Satisfied with her stunned silence, he began unbuttoning her blouse while she stood motionless. Just as he slid the blouse from her shoulders, the photographer arrived noisily in the outer room with his equipment, and Roan groaned in exasperation. "He's early. In there." He waved toward a door at the far end of the room, and needing no second invitation, Analisa bolted past him with her blouse clutched in one hand and her beach bag in the other into an elegantly appointed washroom done in restful shades of lettuce, mint and apple-leaf greens.

With rubbery fingers she tore off her clothes and stepped into the swimsuit, a black figure-hugging maillot with only an elegant curve of shirring from navel to thigh to offset its plainness. She had pulled it as far as her waist when the door swung open and she whirled to turn her back, only to find herself facing a mirror in which she could see Roan standing in the doorway. His eyes, obscured by the black crescents of his half-lowered lashes, were obviously focused on her pink-tipped breasts. Marshalling his anger and impatience, Roan faced her in the mirror and said harshly, "If I wanted a model who looks half-dead, I could have rented a plaster mannequin for ten dollars all day. What I want is a live woman!"

He moved close behind her and reached to pull the swimsuit into place, but as his hands brushed her breasts they lingered, and he pulled her hard back against himself. "Ah, that's better," he commented, viewing her flushed face in the mirror. "I need a woman who looks as if she's just been made love to. I expect the best way to achieve that is by making love to her." He pushed the fabric back down to her waist, his strong hands fondling her until her loins began a slow burn. One hand released a breast to push aside the heavy fall of her hair, exposing the creamy nape of her neck to his searching lips. His other hand slid seductively down her side to her hipbone beneath the satiny black fabric, his massaging palm flat against her taut stomach. Analisa tried to summon her willpower, but the heat that had been creeping up her body burst into a series of explosive, devastating flames until she felt like a pillar of fire and could stand no more. Turning in his arms, she clung to Roan shamelessly, riding demandingly against the hard saddle of his thighs, her breasts softly inviting against his chest.

"Roan," she murmured, lost to all reason. She lifted her face, and he kissed her, teasingly at first and then hungrily until her eyes shone with the languor of her emotions and her lips swelled beneath the pressure of his. Suddenly, he put her away from him to study her with objective impersonality.

"There, that should do it," he announced with satisfaction, and with quick, efficient movements he straightened her maillot and ushered her into the other room where the photographer was set up and waiting.

The photographer was young and brazen, his approving eyes making Analisa feel as though she had stepped under a pair of powerful spotlights. If he was as skilled as he was brash, then he should produce some excellent pictures. "Very sexy!" he commented, and Analisa was aware of a thunderous look from Roan just before he turned away to open a vault and remove the necklace and earrings she was to model. "I see what you mean, de la Corte," continued the reckless young man. "A girl in a bikini wouldn't stand a chance against this. A girl in the *nude* wouldn't stand a chance against this!" Analisa prayed for him to shut up. Standing quietly before Roan while he fastened an ebony and gold necklace about her throat and threaded through her ears the same ebony and gold earrings that she'd originally modeled for Jules Goldfarb, she sensed controlled anger in his body despite the calmness of his face.

As the photographer went to work, arranging and rearranging lights and foils, posing Analisa this way and that, Roan returned to his workbench, concentrating with an intensity that made him oblivious to all the furor around him. When the pictures were later developed, the number one choice of everyone was an unplanned shot the photographer had snapped of Analisa watching Roan at his work, the memory of his recent lovemaking poignant in her face.

It was noon when the session ended, and as soon as the photographer had packed up his gear and departed, Roan brought her clothes from the washroom and ordered crisply, "Change here while I make a phone call. After lunch, you're free to do as you please the rest of the day. I won't be home tonight."

"And what do you propose I do with myself this evening?" She tried to sound aloof, but a slight quaver in her voice made her sound forlorn instead.

"Anything you like, as long as it doesn't involve other men," he replied, adding unkindly, "Surely you can entertain yourself for one evening! Or does your own company bore you as much as it bores me?" He strode from the room, leaving the door ajar, and when Analisa followed to close it, he snapped, reaching for the phone, "Leave it open."

She stood irresolutely a moment, seeking a private corner out of view. Finally, sighing in surrender, she remained directly in his line of vision, skimming the maillot from her slim body to stand motionless and naked a moment before him. Then, with the paradoxical innocence of a child and gracefulness of a beautiful woman who accepts that she is desirable, she slowly dressed. Had she not been so sunk in her own misery, she would have seen Roan's anguish and the gripping whiteness of his knuckles as he hung up the phone without completing the call.

She was folding the swimsuit into its bag when she heard Luisa Costenza's trilling voice in the next room. "Roan darling! I just couldn't wait until tonight to see you, so I've decided to join you for lunch. My treat."

Analisa froze where she was, head bent, afraid of what she might see if she should look up. She had humbled herself naked before him, and now there was greater humiliation to come. There was a brief silence, and then Roan said cheerily, "Sounds great. Just give me a minute to reschedule my plans."

Analisa squared her shoulders, lifted her chin, and stepped into the room before Roan could be the one to jilt her. A minute ago, in that exquisitely painful moment of standing naked before him, she had tacitly offered herself to Roan, but he could rot in Hell if he ever thought she would beg! The blaze in her eyes muted somewhat when she saw her rival's faultless afternoon gown and handmade Italian pumps. Roan watched the silent exchange of animosity with satisfaction, a small complacent smile curving his sensuous mouth.

Analisa's voice was under control, but her face was taut and her eyes were filled with fury as she said casually, "Well, Roan, *darling*," her voice pinched with sarcasm, "I'm on my way, or I'll be late for my appointment. See you sometime."

She whisked from the room, and just before the door closed behind her, she heard Luisa's satisfied laugh. "Just like an outraged wife! I can't believe you picked a dud, Roan, but you must have, to have tired of her in less than a week!"

"Shut up, Luisa!" he snapped, but Analisa was too far down the hall to hear.

She hadn't had breakfast and now she omitted lunch, going straight to the school. As often as she could, Analisa assisted Arvilla Conover, an older, accredited teacher, with her small class of disturbed children. Although Analisa had had no formal training, she—like her mother before her—had a feeling for children that sometimes accomplished more than any textbook theory ever could.

Everything else had gone wrong for Analisa that day, and school was not to be any different. The moment she entered the room where Miss Conover was attempting to retain some sort of order, ten-year-old Freddy leaped from his seat and rushed at her. "You promised to come Monday. You promised!" he shrieked, and before she could react, he had launched a vicious attack on her ankle with his hard-toed shoes. Despite searing pain, she exchanged a triumphant glance with Miss Conover over the boy's head. These were the first words they had heard Freddy speak since his distraught mother had dumped him, an apathetic bundle of expensive, well-cut clothes, at their doorstep six months before. "Do something with him!" she had demanded. "He just quit talking a couple of months ago, and I can't stand this mummified silence another day. Don't send him home until he *will* talk!"

By the time the school day ended, Analisa had a debilitating headache. Despite her determination to be unmoved by Roan's callous treatment of her, she couldn't force herself to go home to his empty house. She tried to eat some supper at a coffee shop, but succeeded only in swallowing some coffee. She took herself to a double feature and sat unseeing through both movies twice. It was nearly midnight when she reached home, feeling wretched and barely able to stand on her swollen, injured foot, and Roan was still not there. She had no idea when he returned, only that it must have been some time after three, when she had finally slept.

She saw nothing of him Saturday, for he was gone before she awakened. She was relieved to note that his bed had been slept in, but he didn't come home when the store closed at noon. He may have stayed on to work in his studio, she surmised. Or he might be with Luisa Costenza again.

Sick at heart, and in too much pain to walk far on her injured foot, Analisa doctored herself with too many aspirins and passed the day in a state of semiconsciousness wondering, guiltily, if this was the kind of anguish that had driven her father to liquor. She longed to call her father, but Roan had forbidden it, so she did not.

She was pouring herself a cup of coffee late Sunday morning when Roan put in an appearance, wearing jeans and a scarlet turtleneck. She had never seen him attired so casually, and the wild thumping of her heart told her that it suited him as much as business or evening dress. Was there anything in which he would not look superb?

"Spending the day in?" she asked, striving to convey neither more nor less than casual interest.

He looked at her oddly. "No, as a matter of fact. I'm going to look for agate out at Painted Rock."

She waited, hoping to be extended an invitation, and when none was issued, asked with feigned nonchalance, "Taking Luisa Costenza?"

He smiled tightly. "Luisa isn't the only girl in the world."

She felt as if her stomach would collapse. "Would you like me to pack you a picnic lunch—for two?"

"Don't you care that I'm taking another girl?" he taunted.

She lifted her head proudly and smiled at him with the same mockery in her eyes with which he'd so often favored her. "A girl other than Luisa? Or other than me? Should I care?" she asked, and knew by the tiny pulsing of his jawline that she'd struck home. Yet she felt no triumph as she stood up and limped to the refrigerator to take out food for his lunch.

His eyes strayed to her ankle, now angrily blue. "Looks like you tangled with a bear trap there," he commented caustically. "And no, I don't want you to fix us a lunch. I don't want you to do *anything* for me."

"Not even stay out of other men's beds?" she purred sweetly and was at once gratified—and alarmed—by the rage burning in his eyes.

Wordlessly he left the room and the house. She didn't see him again until Tuesday night, though she knew by the condition of his bed each morning that he was sleeping at home, arriving late and leaving early.

Her days developed a sameness. She lived in a kind of suspended animation in which she read too much and slept too little, ate nothing and lost weight. She spoke politely to the housekeeper, attended her duties punctiliously at restaurant and school and swam several times daily in the heated pool. Each night she would lie awake hoping for some small change, some sign of relentment from Roan; every morning she would wake up alone in the silent house. Already she regretted displeasing him—how much would he make her suffer?

Unable to endure the sudden cessation of conversation whenever she entered the restaurants, she hired Jeanette and Juan and left her job the first week of November, a week earlier than Roan had stipulated. Rising early the next morning after her resignation, she confronted Roan at breakfast—the first time she'd seen him in days. Quietly she requested that she be allowed to take over all of Ardith's duties and run the house herself. Roan's expression, already closed, became cold. "No doubt it has not occurred to you," he sneered, "that Ardith needs the income the job provides."

"And I need some activity to keep my blood from freezing in this—this polar air!" she shouted, disgusted with herself for the tears that shimmered on her lashes.

"Bored with yourself already, Analisa?"

"Yes, I'm bored with myself!" she raged. "I'm too ashamed to face any of my old girl friends, and you won't allow me the company of men. If—if humiliation is the coin in which you intend to collect, then don't you think my debt is fully paid?"

"Humiliation is *not* the coin, and you know it!" He pushed his mug savagely away, sloshing coffee onto the countertop, and stamped from the room. Yes, he meant to force her to her knees. He would make her beg.

Analisa sat in the kitchen and heard the front door slam. She asked herself why she remained his captive, taking this emotional and spiritual abuse. It wasn't because she had no job and no place to go, nor even because she knew that Roan would only find her and bring her back, although all these things were true. It was because she loved him. No matter where she went, she would still and always be his captive, the prisoner of her own ransomed heart.

"We're going to a ball at the Costenza's Saturday night," Roan announced cheerfully a few nights later, having come home early in a rare fine humor.

"We?" she asked nervously. "You *can't* expect me to go there?" Incredulity outweighed her anger.

"Expect?" He raised one eyebrow. "I insist. Get yourself a new gown and charge it to me."

"No," she refused flatly. "It would only put me deeper in your debt."

"Then take it out of the bank account I opened for you."

"I haven't touched that, and I have no intention of doing so—for reasons above stated," she added sarcastically. "There's nothing wrong with the gowns I already have."

"Suit yourself." He shrugged, dismissing her.

She wore a long-sleeved silver lamé sheath, slit, of necessity, to just above the knee to allow unimpeded dancing. The shoulders were gathered to form a broad square neckline, the gown was totally without adornment. When Roan came through the hall from his own room, his warm smile of approval was music for her heart to dance by. He opened a rectangular box which she recognized immediately, and fastened about her neck the sapphire necklace which had originally delivered her to him as his chattel. Lifting her shimmering tresses he kissed the back of her neck with calculated intent. She half expected him to produce the sapphire and diamond ring, too, but as if reading her thoughts he said with a superior smile, "No rings of any kind, Analisa. I want the world to

102

know you're mine and after tonight it surely will. But heaven forbid anyone should think you're my wife or my fiancée. You see, contrary to your belief, the trapper is not trapped."

She closed her eyes against annihilating pain, reaching out blindly to touch him. He remained aloof and silent and, withdrawing her hand, she opened her eyes to stare at him resentfully. "Please, Roan, can't we be nice to each other just for tonight?"

He took her in his arms, his lips playing with her hair, his breath warmly tantalizing against her cheek. "Tonight, we shall be more than nice to each other. While all of Valley society watches, intrigued, we shall be entranced with one another." She shuddered, and he put her from him. "One more thing." He left her a moment to return with a delicate corsage of lily-of-the-valley, pinning it to her shoulder while she stood captivated by the touch of his hand upon her breast.

"Lily-of-the-valley? How did you manage that at this time of year?" She gave him a dazzling smile. "And why lily-of-the-valley, instead of something more conventional?"

"Florists are amazing people," he smiled, his eyes kindling at her obvious pleasure. "Just as your father should have given you emeralds instead of sapphires for your May birthday, I offer you lily-of-the-valley. The May stone, the May flower, for a May beauty." He offered his arm. "Come. Let us dance and pretend to be merry."

By midevening, their pleasure in one another no longer seemed a pretense. Roan showered her with amorous attention, sharing at least half her dances, while Luisa pouted in the background. Even when

Roan was not in attendance, Analisa didn't lack for partners. She was overjoyed by his attentiveness, certain that the coldness between them need never be repeated, and foolishly she let her pleasure shine in her eyes, as Roan had intended it should. She knew that she and Roan were the center of conversation by the comments made openly in front of her, but she had no idea what was being said behind her back until a blond young skyscraper who had repeatedly cut in on her dances enlightened her. It was nearly midnight, and drinks had flowed freely, loosening tongues. The young man, whose name she thought was Robert, had held her for two consecutive dances, and as the music began on yet another fox trot, he deftly guided her into a shadowed corner behind a huge rubber tree, where he pinned her with a hand to the wall on each side of her, smiling confidently. "There's a pervasive rumor going around the hall that you are de la Corte's *very* personal property. You must be a recent acquisition, considering he's been seen almost every night for the past month with our host's beautiful granddaughter. Well, foxy lady, next time he shafts you, let's you and me deal it back to him. What do you say, gorgeous?"

All pleasure drained from the evening and from her face. Her eyes blazed. "If you're so quick to believe that I am Roan's *very* private property, perhaps you'd do well to respect his right of ownership. Certainly you don't think I could turn to someone like you after experiencing Roan's lovemaking!" The words galled her, but she desperately wanted to break free, and reasoned that a good insult would send him away. But she had misjudged him.

Her partner's placid face turned ugly, and one hand moved to squeeze her breast in angry, painful retaliation. In the next instant, he was spun from her, knocking into the rubber tree and sliding to the floor in a semi-conscious heap.

"Oh, Roan!" Analisa cried, flinging herself against his chest in genuine relief.

"Well said, my *lover*," he commented dryly. The rigidness of his body as she clung to him told her he was as angry with her as he had been with her adversary. "You must have seen me coming to put on such an act of outrage." She looked at him startled, and fell back as he continued, "I notice you let him monopolize your last few dances. What kind of *encouragement* did you give him that you have never given me?"

"Roan, you can't mean that!"

"Get your wrap, Analisa, and wait for me in the front entry."

As ordered, she huddled into her mink jacket in a dark corner of the vestibule. She heard Luisa's irritating laugh, and a moment later Luisa and Roan emerged arm-in-arm from the adjacent room. The instant she thought they were alone, Luisa wrapped her arms about Roan and kissed him long and ardently. It seemed to Analisa there was something dispassionate about the careless way Roan responded to her embrace. At least she told herself it was so. When she could stand it no longer, she stepped out of the shadows to confront them silently. Unperturbed, Luisa took a handkerchief from her bag and wiped her lipstick from Roan's mouth.

"There you are," Roan said without embarrassment. "We'll drop you off, then Luisa and I are going on to an all-night discotheque."

CHAPTER 7

THEY DROVE home with Luisa wedged cozily in the middle against Roan, her hand resting possessively on his knee as he drove. Analisa, seated on the outside, had the car door open and was halfway out even before the car had stopped in the driveway. She landed precariously, a sharp pain in her weakened ankle bringing her almost to her knees upon impact, but then she was up and running. Behind her she heard Luisa's high tinkle of laughter as she leaned out to close the gaping car door, and her lighthearted, "Frankly, darling, if you treated me that way, I'd kill you. What a dolt she must be to put up with you!"

The tears she had fought for so long now flowed freely, hour after hour of them, until her head was swollen to bursting, her breathing congested, her stomach churning and heaving. The moon waned, sun shone, the moon came again. Lying semiconscious on her bed, her reinjured ankle swollen painfully, she lost all track of time. At some point during her isolation, the tears subsided, bled dry, and when the tear-fed swelling went out of her face it was replaced by gauntness. She knew only one thing: Roan didn't come home, which meant that he had already moved some of his things into Luisa's apartment. A man as fastidious as Roan de la Corte didn't live three days in the same set of underwear.

Her thoughts went round and round. He had said she must beg, so he could have the pleasure of rejecting her. But beg she would *not!* She would leave him. Just as soon as she found the strength to move off her bed. How many days would it be before he would even realize she had gone? She could no longer cry, so she laughed mirthlessly, silently. She was aware at one time of Ardith fussing over her, then another period of isolation, more fussing.

Suddenly the darkened room filled with light. "In bed at this time of evening?" asked a familiar voice.

Her heart gave a feeble thud, as a sick-unto-death puppy might thump his tail at the sound of his beloved master's voice. "What time?" she asked weakly, rolling onto her stomach to hide her gaunt face in the pillow.

"Seven P.M."

"What day?" Her voice was muffled by the bedding.

"Wednesday." Suddenly Roan's angry hands were on her shoulders, turning her over. He recoiled from the sight of her thin, bloodless face, the opaque, exhausted eyes. "My God!" He became very still, assessing her with penetrating eyes. "What have you been doing to yourself, Analisa?" Suspicion had replaced the shock in his voice.

"Nothing. But I will. *For* myself. I'm going to leave you, Roan." Idiotic threat—*he* had already left *her*. "Your house," she amended.

The pulse jumped whitely from hard jaw to temple. "Don't even try it, Analisa. I'll only find you and bring you back. Save yourself the embarrassment."

She rolled again onto her stomach, and presently she heard him opening and closing drawers in bedroom and bath, slamming them harder as his agitation mounted. She sat up to watch, curious, her seventy-pound head braced painfully in her hands. "What are you doing?"

"Where is it?" he demanded. "What have you been taking?"

"If I'd wanted to kill myself, I'd have succeeded!" she shot at him with all her ebbing strength. "Surely you don't believe I consider you worth committing suicide over?" Why hadn't she thought of that? She asked, "Why did you come back?"

"Ardith called to say I'd better. She doesn't approve of the way we live, but she didn't want to be the one to come upon the body." He might have been discussing bad weather.

Nevertheless, he stayed close for several days, aloofly kind but never tender, coaxing her back to health if not vigor, to acceptance if not cheerfulness. She regained some of her lost weight, though her eyes retained their haunted look. Sometimes she would see Roan studying her keenly, but he'd turn away, wincing, when he found he'd been caught in his appraisal. They spent silent evenings in the library, he preoccupied at his desk, she pouring over books, usually Paris de la Corte's texts on child psychiatry or physical therapy or music, all subjects that particularly interested her. Her mind would go blank, and she'd find herself watching Roan, his dark head bent over his work, his beautiful, capable hands occupied at the sketch pad. Then the tumult would begin in her stomach, the terrible pain of need and deprivation that no surgeon's knife could excise. Once Roan touched her shoulder, and she had shivered from the driving need it aroused. Misunderstanding, he had withdrawn his hand quickly, and he'd never touched her again. If only he hadn't told her it was useless to beg!

She was stronger now, physically and emotionally better able to cope with the fragments of her life. Never again would she allow herself to be so vulnerable, to be thrown into the neurotic state in which Roan's defection to Luisa had left her. No matter what Roan's objections might be, it was time for her to regain control of her own life.

Analisa had once dreamed of getting a degree in business from the University of Arizona, but had given up that idea when her mother had died—there had been her mother's place to fill at the restaurants, her father's dependency upon her, and her work again in her mother's place, at the school. She had known after only three visits that no major could ever give her more satisfaction than the knowledge that with her help a child might overcome his learning drawback sufficiently to enter public school and eventually become a self-sufficient citizen. When she'd started as an unpaid volunteer, no educational credits were required of her; and three years ago she would not have dreamed that her financial future—the restaurants she expected one day to inherit—would ever be threatened. At that time, advanced education had not been important. Not so any more.

She told Roan she wanted to go to school. "I can always get a job as cook, but somehow I don't see myself working in other peoples' restaurants. I'd like to expand my work with children. With a major in special education and a minor in psychophysics—"

He stared at her stonily, his silver eyes unreadable. "I don't see you working anywhere, except as a volunteer as you're doing now." He spoke with finality, but she chose to argue.

"I must learn now to make my own way, as eventually I will have to do!"

"You'll always be provided for, Analisa." This time the decisiveness in his voice silenced her. But now that she had once again shown her mettle, her determination was only toughened by his obstinacy. She couldn't start classes until the January quarter, but nevertheless she enrolled in a course on child development at Arizona State to begin then, making no secret of her rebellious intention. Gradually they drifted apart as Roan stayed away more and more evenings and Analisa became cold and formal with him.

One afternoon in early December he announced, "I've finally found a trained manager for the Nob Hill shop. Trenton Westfield will arrive from San Francisco next week to resume his apprenticeship with me. He'll be staying here with us until he finds a place of his own."

She smiled derisively. "And will you continue staying out late every night, leaving me alone with him?"

His hands gripped her shoulders in a painful vise. "He has a fiancée who will be following as soon as he's settled. Leave him alone!"

"I'm sorry," she murmured, genuinely contrite. "That was spiteful of me."

His grip relaxed, becoming almost tender, and a weakness in her knees grew into a longing in her loins. "He's twenty-six, attractive, intelligent, with a certain charisma of his own. But I'm warning you, I'll not be cuckolded—"

There was a sad vulnerability in her smile and in her sea-green eyes. Softly she asked, "How can I cuckold you when I've never belonged to you, Roan?"

He said the wrong thing, his eyes narrowed. "You've not begged me, Analisa." The tenderness left her face, her eyes clouded over with an opaque screen. It was like watching someone die.

Trenton Westfield, a little shorter than Roan but as broad-shouldered, had brown hair and dark, friendly brown eyes; a brown beard she wished he didn't have because she suspected it hid a firm, attractive chin, and a crooked nose that looked as if it had been broken at some time in a fight—although she doubted that, since a man born to be a goldsmith would be as protective of his hands as a surgeon or a concert pianist. Roan watched their meeting with hooded eyes, and stayed close all that weekend. Although Analisa's first reaction was one of immediate liking, and she at once felt confident of his integrity, she could not imagine her feelings for the newcomer ever developing into anything beyond deep affection.

Trenton arrived on a Saturday, and on Sunday there was a dinner party to introduce him to important members of the trade, almost all of whom were as unknown to their hostess as they were to Trenton. Analisa looked forward to the event with great delight. They called upon Ardith to clean the house and wait table, freeing Analisa to cook the dinner, which she did magnificently. Cooking was therapeutic to her battered ego, and it was pleasant to be of some use again. Afterward Ardith cleaned up, and Analisa remained with the guests. She was relieved that the guest list didn't include the voluptuous Luisa, but found that her absence did not altogether alleviate tension. In spite of everything Analisa could do for them—and she was an accomplished hostess—the guests remained uncomfortable. She could only conclude they were aware of her position as Roan's alleged co-mistress, and she was glad when the evening ended at last.

Trenton had been assigned a room in the guest wing on the opposite side of the house from their own suite, a subtle reminder that he was an outsider. In the mornings the two men usually left for work together, though Trenton had his own car. Therefore, on the evenings that Roan didn't come home, neither did his understudy. Out with the boys, Analisa told herself the first time it happened, or maybe working late. But when she caught Trent off-guard in an intense, bewildered scrutiny of herself, she knew it was not so. The guilt and compassion in his gentle brown eyes and the compression of his thin lips told her he knew—and did not approve—of Roan's behavior. But if he was engaged, how did his fiancée in San Francisco fit into these nocturnal activities? Did he simply go along as odd man out? She doubted that!

Analisa asked Trent one day when his fiancée would be joining him. He greeted her question with surprise. "Polly? Not until our house is completed and we're in a position to set a date. Though of course she'll fly in for visits when she can. She's coming for Christmas, in fact. Roan has already extended her a personal invitation to stay here." But he hadn't said anything to Analisa so she could prepare a room and plan her menus around a fourth. But most likely, Polly would dine out and be entertained royally by her fiancé and by Roan and his lover—while she herself stayed at home like the maid. No, not like the maid. Like nothing—for she soon learned Ardith had already been advised to prepare for another guest, while she herself would have been left uninformed had it not been for Trenton's apprisal.

Christmas was almost upon them when Paris de la Corte, encountering Analisa at school, uncharacteristically invited her for a cup of coffee when their work was done. Obviously something was on her mind, and nervously, Analisa accepted.

Mrs. de la Corte lit a cigarette, leaned back and puffed out a cloud of smoke while they waited for service. "Roan hates me to smoke. Do you mind?" Analisa smiled diffidently, not knowing how to answer. "You do mind." With a throaty chuckle, she stamped the cigarette out in the glass ashtray. "You're both smarter than I am. About some things."

Analisa flushed slightly at the inference and shifted her curious gaze away. The woman's grey eyes reminded her of Roan's, except that they were readable and sympathetic, if not actually warm. She thought the black hair was probably retrieved from grey, though so expertly no one could be certain. Apart from the eyes, the round face, carefully made up to subtract years, showed no resemblance to her son's, who looked much more like his father. Analisa wondered if, in his younger days, the old man had been as fickle as his son. Certainly Paris de la Corte didn't look like a discontented woman.

"Roan tells me you were quite ill. I doubt you've fully recovered, although he tells me you have. Men are so blind." The coffee arrived, and she took a sip, giving Analisa a chance to reply—an opportunity she declined to utilize. Paris went on, "At least it got him out of *our* hair! We love our son, but there's something vulgar about a twenty-eight-year-old man coming home to Mama."

Analisa's heart thudded painfully. "Y-you mean he was staying with you?" she gulped.

"Where else? Surely you didn't think he was living with Luisa Costenza? I doubt he could take her in such large doses." Analisa's expressive eyes gave silent thanks for the small reprieve. "I thought for a while it was finally over between them, but I see it hasn't ended yet. She must be in his blood, like gambling." Analisa's color rose in anger and despair at the thoughtless remark, even though she was sure Paris had spoken carelessly with no intent to hurt or humiliate.

The older woman started to take a bite of shortcake, then suddenly returned her fork to her plate. "You're not happy, Analisa. Why don't you leave him? He has no legal hold on you." Analisa shook her head dumbly. "Then the rumors are true. I could slit Luisa's throat."

At last Analisa found her voice. "Why Luisa's? She had to have got her information from Roan."

"Not Roan!" his mother defended sharply. "Roan would never have done anything so vicious. Luisa was in an excellent position to put two and two together, and her mouth, believe me, is even bigger than her ego. I am, frankly, neither fond nor proud of my cousin's granddaughter." She swallowed more coffee, then said, "He can't hold you as his chattel, you know. There are laws against it. Leave him, Analisa, while you're still a virgin."

The woman's practicality and percipience left her

gasping. "No," she finally demurred. "I can't do that."

"Ah," her companion sighed regretfully. "You're in love with him. What a fool the man is!"

Polly Austen—pretty, sensible and cheerful—arrived that evening. Having had a small part of her dignity restored by her interview with Paris de la Corte, Analisa was less frigid with Roan than usual. Whether because of this or for Polly's benefit, she was not excluded from any of the holiday activities. On Christmas Eve they all attended a gala ball at the recently completed civic center. Christmas day itself Roan reserved for "immediate family," which for the moment necessarily included their house-guests, and Analisa took immense satisfaction in turning out a festive Christmas dinner which Guiglo, slowly recovering from his heart surgery, and Paris de la Corte praised without restraint. Analisa had been surprised and pleased to learn that Polly was an old-fashioned girl who still lived with her parents and planned to continue doing so until her wedding day. There was an instant affinity between the two girls.

On Christmas morning, Roan slipped into the kitchen while Analisa was preparing breakfast before their guests were up. Pulling her arm playfully behind her he clamped something to her wrist. "Merry Christmas, Analisa," he murmured, kissing her nape before releasing her wrist. She stared at the beautiful bracelet he had fastened there, a wide, open-work clip of desert leaves and stems in black onyx with a three-dimensional single rose blossom of pink gold.

"The desert rose!" she whispered in delighted awe.

"I hope you like it. I had the devil's own time coming up with a gold alloy of exactly the right shade."

"*Like* it!" she cried. "Oh, Roan, is it all right to cry now, it's so beautiful!" He held her head to his chest, where she could hear the hard, steady beat of his heart. When she looked up at him, her eyes were shining with happiness, yet there were tears of sadness shimmering there, too. She touched his cheek apologetically, loving the smooth-shaven firmness of his jaw. "I'm sorry, Roan. I didn't get you anything. The only thing I could think of—isn't available."

He raised one eyebrow inquiringly. "What might that have been?"

She hesitated before confessing, "A heart." Then she added quickly, "But perhaps someone else has given you one, you've been so kind these past few days."

There was a moment of pain in his eyes before an obscuring cloud slipped into place like an obedient servant. "Couldn't you have given me yours?"

She caught her breath. "It's already been given, Roan."

She reached out to touch him again, but he stepped sharply out of reach. "You didn't tell me. You never once suggested you had a lover!"

She wanted to cry out, "No! You misunderstood, Roan!" but before she could speak, the cold, protective mask had fallen into place, hiding his feelings and protecting his—God help her, protecting his pride? Was pride all that held them apart?

Polly returned to San Francisco, and Trenton continued his search for an affordable apartment to lease until his house was completed. And at some indefinable moment there had been a turning point in the relationship between Roan and Analisa, for Roan began actively courting her. A certain restraint, a kind of deference, remained between them, but now when he took her out—as he frequently did—his concern for her happiness seemed genuine and not just a performance for the benefit of an audience. Together they attended ballet, concerts, Phoenix Little Theatre productions and sporting events, discovering between themselves an ever more delightful compatibility. Recalling Roan's contempt for the single-mindedness of the sexually hungry woman, Analisa sometimes thought, ruefully, that the bedroom was the only thing they didn't have in common. True, they continued to share adjoining rooms, on which the connecting doors were never closed, but Roan made no unwanted advances—though deep in her heart, Analisa knew there was no such thing as an unwanted advance from Roan. They picnicked and rock-hounded on the winter desert, and swam exuberantly in the pool, where each time she had to defend her right not to wear a bikini. Once when she was floating on her back, he swam over her, his chest hard and intimidating against her soft breasts, and teased, "Why not a bikini? Have you forgotten that you once showed me your whole beautiful body?"

And he had turned straight from the sight of it to Luisa Costenza's arms. No, she hadn't forgotten.

December became January, and Roan sent her off to her daily classes at ASU with his blessing, no longer crippling her right to self-expression. These days Analisa was radiantly beautiful, yet there always lurked in her eyes a shadow of sadness. She dared not let herself forget the emotional price she had paid for her present happiness—nor could she forget that, while she and Roan were no longer at odds, neither was their relationship complete.

Orlando Avalon's restaurant in Tempe had folded on New Year's Day, and more recently he had been forced to sell the Phoenix operation to Juan and Jeanette Ortiz, the chefs to whom Analisa had entrusted the family recipes. Only one left now. How long before that, too, would go?

The first time she had gone to Roan's office to meet him for lunch, Analisa had been flattered to see an oval-framed photograph of herself on his desk. Her pale face was set against a solid aquamarine background that picked up the color of her eyes and drew the viewer's attention almost hypnotically to the black and gold jewelry at her throat and ears. Her face, she knew, held the look of a woman who had just been made love to and who loved, yet at the same time it expressed virginal purity. She had blushed, remembering Roan's hands upon her unresisting body, his lips caressing hers, remembering where her attention had been when the photographer had captured that look. "When did you get this?" she had asked in pleased surprise.

"Surely you remember when it was made," he answered with mock astonishment.

"Of course. But I hadn't expected to see it here. In fact, you never did tell me its original purpose."

He laughed as he stroked the picture the way she often wished he would stroke her body. "You're a remarkably incurious girl. It has recently appeared in ads in a number of the finest magazines—*Town & Country, Gourmet, Vogue, Glamour*—but of course, the first picture out of the lab was mine."

Sometimes in the social whirl Analisa encountered Roan's ex-mistress and was aware of her hate-filled eyes following her every move, but she no longer feared Luisa Costenza. Occasionally, rarely, Roan had to work late, but Trenton always backed him up on his alibi. Because Analisa had the deepest respect for Trenton's integrity, she never doubted his word. Therefore she was caught completely off-guard when the worst happened.

Roan and Analisa were attending a fund-raising ball when she excused herself to go to the powder room. She was in one of the stalls when the outer door opened and, after a brief pause, she heard Luisa say, "I hate having to take a later plane than Roan's, but you've seen how possessive Analisa is. She scarcely lets the poor darling out of her sight. She'll undoubtedly insist upon driving him to the airport Monday, and it wouldn't do for us to be seen there together." There was no reply, and Analisa had the uncanny feeling that Luisa was out there performing alone. *She followed me here deliberately,* Analisa told herself. *She recognized my shoes beneath the door.* Analisa had asked Roan to make her some diamond clips to accentuate the simple elegance of her black pumps, and consequently her shoes had been the rage of the ball. At midnight the clips were to be auctioned as the de la Corte family's contribution to the Heart Fund.

Dancing with Roan shortly after that, she asked as innocently as she could manage about his proposed trip, and he admitted, disconcertedly, that he was going to New York City for a few days. And no, it wasn't necessary for her to drive him to the airport; he preferred to leave his car on the long-term lot, convenient for his return. "I didn't want to tell you until my plans were firm," he said without apparent guile, "and somehow, I couldn't face the possibility that you might not be totally desolated by my departure."

"Oh, I am desolated, Roan," she murmured. "I am desolated."

The freeze had set in again, but this time Roan was the victim and he hadn't the slightest idea why. When the dance ended, Analisa excused herself distractedly and wandered alone to the buffet in the adjoining room. She piled her plate with food she couldn't bear to eat, not really knowing that she did so, and went to sit in a shadowy corner behind a planter of palms. She stared unseeing at the food in her lap. Roan had been lying to her again, and Trenton had lied for him.

On the other side of the planter, a woman's voice was saying, "I frankly can't understand why she stays with him—unless Luisa's little rumor is more true than I like to believe. She's the marrying kind if ever I saw such a girl, but to live in his house while he squires about that despicable Costenza girl—"

A strident voice interrupted, "I'd say they're two of a kind. *She's* living with *two* men, so who knows what she's up to while he's out with Luisa? Though I can't say as I blame her, the way Roan flaunted that temptress all those months."

The voices drifted away, and Analisa consulted her watch. In another half hour, the auction was to begin. She set her plate among the palms and went in search of Roan. Her hands, as white as her face, were shaking as she removed the diamond clips from her pumps and handed them to Roan. "Here. It's almost time."

"Analisa!" he cried, clasping the hands that held the jewels out to him. "For God's sake, what's happened? You look ill!"

Wordlessly she pulled her hands from his and walked away. Out in the cold February night, she hailed a cab and sped away.

CHAPTER 8

To HER relief, all was in darkness when the cab stopped before the house. She walked softly through the unlighted rooms, not wanting to disturb Trenton asleep in his quarters at the opposite side of the house. Because her room seemed unusually cold, Analisa changed into a heavy satin gown instead of one of her usual filmy ensembles. Mechanically she sat down before her vanity. Her white, anguished reflection stared back at her. So it was all beginning again. What a fool she had been! Since that night she had rejected him, Roan had curbed his masculine passion, but for almost two months now the concern, the tenderness had been there. Surely that was what mattered in a long-term relationship. She had allowed herself to believe that he was proving himself, giving her time to learn to trust him before asking her to marry him. In a few months, she would be twenty-two. She was innocent, but she was not naïve; she had dated many men, both younger and older than Roan, and she knew the difference between love and infatuation. What she didn't understand was why her heart, in defiance of the most basic logic, had given itself to a two-timing

122

amorosa like Roan de la Corte. She buried her face in her trembling hands and wished for the comfort of tears, but none came.

"I hate him, I hate him, *I hate him!*" she ground out; but the lie wouldn't wash. The harder she willed the pain to go away, the more intense it became. "Oh, Daddy," she asked the empty room, "is this anything like the pain you've felt these past few months? Did my leaving hurt you like this? Is that why you crawled into a bottle and began to die?"

She made her way across the darkened hall, down the three steps to the center level and into the kitchen, where she turned on one panel of the ceiling lights. In one of the cupboards she recalled seeing a nearly full fifth of bourbon left from the holidays. She found it, took a water tumbler from the dish cabinet, and lifted the bottle high, staring through the light at its amber promise of anesthesia. "Move over, Daddy," she said, the softness of her voice not hiding the hysteria in it. "I'm coming in with you."

"Analisa! What are you doing here?"

She stepped back involuntarily, hugging the bottle defensively to her chest, and stared into Trenton's shocked eyes. He seemed to tower formidably in the open doorway, hastily tying the belt of his navy dressing gown.

"I might ask you the same thing," she countered with a pathetic attempt at dignity. "I thought you were asleep. Why did you lie to me, Trent?"

He crossed the room and with a swift, sure movement wrested the bottle and glass gently from her, pushing them to the back of the counter. "I've never lied to you in my life."

"Don't. *Don't!*" Anguish pierced her voice. "You

told me he was working, and all the time he was with *her* again!"

"I swear to you he was working!" Pain slashed across his face. He stood in front of her, cracking his knuckles as if he'd prefer to crack someone's head.

"He's taking her to New York with him Monday. I overheard her telling someone, and when I asked him if he was planning a trip, he admitted it. He said he was only waiting until his p-plans were f-f-firm before telling me. He's leaving day after tomorrow! If they're not firm n-now, when will they be!"

"Oh, God, Analisa! I thought—I wouldn't have believed—" She was in his arms, not knowing how she got there, her head cradled against his shoulder. "Cry, Analisa," he murmured against her hair. "There's therapy in tears."

She lifted her head to stare at him dry-eyed a long moment, then shook her head wistfully. "I spent my tears a long time ago, Trent. Anyway, Roan doesn't like me to cry. I suppose it makes him feel guilty."

"Do you always do as Roan wishes?"

She smiled forlornly. "I try. Though at the very first, I didn't always. Could that have been my mistake?"

"I think the mistakes are all his," Trenton said grimly. "But believe me, lying about his working nights isn't one of them." He hesitated, obviously debating with himself. "No surprise is worth the agony you're going through, Analisa, and though Roan may not easily forgive me, I think you should know the truth. He's been working on a birthday gift for you, and there's been no time to do it during regular hours."

"But my birthday is more than three months away!"

"I know that. And frankly, I don't see how he hopes to have this particular trinket ready before your twenty-third or even twenty-fourth birthday. But then, he's a far superior craftsman to me.

"Now," he said firmly, "I can't explain this New York trip, though I'm sure there is an explanation. But I want you to forget that bottle—it's no solution!—and stop underestimating yourself." One hand moved from her waist to wind itself in her long, silken hair, pulling her head back and forcing her to return his unflinching gaze. His brown eyes were gentle and kind, filled only with compassion as he said, "Forget Luisa. Beside you, she doesn't exist. She's nothing. I do believe you're the only girl in the world who could ever make me forget my lovely, pure Polly."

"Very touching!" The voice in the doorway was savage, the grey eyes glacial above the thin white lips. "So this is where you ran off to—and why!" Analisa would have broken guiltily from Trenton's embrace, but his arm tightened, forbidding it.

"I'm glad something touches you, old boy," Trenton said with deep irony. "Maybe you'd like to explain to both of us why you're planning to tiptoe off to New York on Monday with Luisa."

"What the hell are you talking about?" Roan's eyes blazed as he advanced on the pair.

Trenton shrugged indifferently. "You don't have to convince me of anything, Roan, but maybe you can take your broken toy and put her back together good as new. Before she starts borrowing her father's opiate." With a pointed look at the liquor bottle he released Analisa and stalked angrily from the room.

Roan stared at the bottle in incredulous revulsion. "Oh, my God," he moaned, catching Analisa and pulling her unresistingly to him. Then, in renewed anger, he roared after Trenton's retreating figure, "Westfield, I want you out of this house before I leave!"

Trenton turned to level his employer with contemptuous brown eyes. "I'm one step ahead of you. I'll be moving into a motel tomorrow evening. I'm already packed, and will be out of here by noon." He strode off defiantly.

Roan caught Analisa's limp, slight body up in his arms and carried her gently to her bed. Carefully laying her down, he allowed his hands to drift languidly through her disarrayed locks before standing up and looking down at her with eyes as bleak as a wintry plain.

"Trent knew you were going away. Luisa knew," Analisa said dejectedly. "Why didn't I know?"

"Trenton knows because he's my business associate. I was waiting for my final instructions before speaking to you." He was standing very erect, the stillness of his hands at his sides emphasizing his controlled strength. "I won't have them until tomorrow, as there are rather—extensive last-minute arrangements to be made."

"Yet you've already made your plane reservation for Monday."

"It's easier to cancel a reservation than to make one at the last minute." He stood quietly—waiting for further accusation? When none came, he added with uncharacteristic apathy, "I've no more idea how Luisa learned of my trip than I know how you did. I could tell you she's not going with me, that she's no part of my plans, but I forfeited the right a long time ago to ask you to believe in me. Good night, Analisa." He turned and walked to his own room, his lean body as lithe and silent as a panther.

She wanted to plead, "Deny it, deny it and I'll believe you!" but she knew he never would. She wanted to pursue him to his room, but she knew that if she did she would let him make love to her—and then she would truly be lost.

She heard him moving about in his room, and then his light went out. A few minutes later she heard his car moving on the gravel, a distant sound that dealt a death blow to her hopes. She got up and turned off her own light and lay down again on the round bed. She thought about the blessed promise of oblivion that beckoned from the kitchen. She thought about her father, whom she hadn't seen in a quarter of a year, but whose well-documented degeneration had been, on more than one occasion, callously laid at her feet. Not even Roan de la Corte, she determined, was going to do to her what had been done to her father. Gradually, exhaustion overtook pain, and she slept.

When Analisa woke, Roan was not in his room, and she had no idea if he'd come home. Half a pot of coffee was placed on "warm" in the kitchen, but that may have been Trenton's doing. She poured herself a mug with unsteady hands, then, needing a refuge, carried it to the library, which more than any other room in the house, seemed to suggest an aura of serenity.

She walked in on Roan, seated at his desk listening at the phone. He saw her at once. As she started to back out, he raised a hand, signaling her to remain. His eyes were friendly enough, but there was no welcoming smile on his face.

She walked to the fireplace and deposited her mug on the mantel, her back to Roan. "I'm convinced," she heard him say cryptically, "that's all there was to it. But it also convinces me we should move as quickly as possible. So far, only the rumor that I'm flying to New York has leaked; we'd better get it over with before the purpose is discerned. . . . Right. I'll see you tomorrow then."

He hung up, and she sensed rather than heard his approach. She turned to face him, taking a steadying sip of her coffee, her eyes enormous over the rim of the mug. "I wish I could get out of this trip," he said, "or at least postpone it. I wish—" His hand reached out, then fell to his side. "I wish I had the right to touch you. To—ask you to believe in me." His voice betrayed a vulnerability she'd never before suspected, and a ray of curiosity flickered in her eyes.

"Take me with you, Roan." She was begging now, unashamed. What did her pride matter when he was being so sincere, when they were so close to reaching an understanding?

"No!" The word cut like a rawhide whip, laying her heart open. She replaced her mug very carefully on the mantel and walked past him toward the door. "Analisa!" She stopped, standing still with her back to him. "Please don't let it happen again—what happened the last time I was away. And don't try to leave me. I won't let you go."

She turned slowly to stare at him. After a while, she said quietly, "Don't worry, Roan. I'll be here, sober and in good condition, when you return. But I'll never stop praying for the day you set me free."

A terrible, lacerating anguish flooded his face, but she had already turned away. When she had gone, he sank to his knees and cried for the first time in twenty years.

CHAPTER 9

TRENTON CALLED from the store on Tuesday to ask Analisa if she would come in and help him out with the phones for a few hours in the secretary's absence. Though no secretary herself, she readily agreed, eager to escape her own melancholy company. She had avoided Roan on Sunday by spending the afternoon alone on the desert, huddled against a chilly wind in a lightweight blue windbreaker, talking to no one, seeing no one except for a robust young man perched against the skyline atop a high boulder. He was about a quarter mile behind the house, glassing the rocky hills, a quiver of arrows and a hunting bow strapped to his back. She'd wondered what he might be hunting at this season, finally concluding it could only be rabbits—if one can shoot at something so small with a bow and arrow.

The next morning Analisa had deliberately slept in, giving Roan time to leave for the airport without seeing her and having to maintain his pretense of preferring to stay home. Ardith's maddeningly cheerful loquacity had then driven her out on the desert for another day. She had taken a book, a sketch pad and a small lunch, and for a lonely, friendless girl had spent a tolerable day.

Adjusting the rearview mirror as she drove to the store, she noticed an undistinguished-looking black sedan behind her which seemed to maintain her pace. She stopped at the cleaners on her way to the office, and as she left there, she noticed a similar black car parked across the street. Was she being followed? Had her father, as Roan had feared, found another house where he could gamble? The sedan vanished and she relaxed. Black cars, which in summer soak up unbearable amounts of heat under the blazing desert sun, were unusual in this locale. Winter tourists, she supposed. It was the color alone, she concluded, that had caught her attention.

By the time she reached the office it was nearly noon, and Trenton suggested lunch before settling to work. She hadn't seen him since his dismissal from the house Saturday night, and was uncomfortably aware that he was studying her covertly. Did he expect to find physical bruises on her body? They talked amiably, but it was a relief to return to the store. Analisa settled behind Roan's desk while Trenton proceeded to the workroom. To fill in her time between incoming calls, she brought the ledgers up to date—having had some bookkeeping experience in connection with the restaurants—and filed a tray of correspondence and accounts payable. Late in the afternoon, Trenton gave her a number to dial. "Just ring through," he instructed, "but don't say anything. Listen while I talk. I'll pick it up on Alice's phone across the hall." With the opposing doors open, seated where she had an unobstructed view of him, she was aware of a growing tension in him as the phone rang eight—nine—ten times. After the third futile attempt, she heard him mutter, "I *know* I'm right."

Just before closing time, they made connection, and Analisa stifled a gasp upon recognizing the sultry voice which answered.

"Luisa, pet, I was beginning to think I'd been jilted." Analisa stared in astonishment across the hallway to the young man who was blatantly wooing Roan's lover. She could never in this life have thought of Trenton as a seducer!

"Trenton? Is that you?" Luisa asked uncertainly.

"None other. While the cat's away, dear heart . . ."

"Roan!" she spat with singular scorn. "That bastard! But Trenton honey, let's not talk about the dead—"

"That's a strange turn of phrase, pet." Trenton had paled several shades as Analisa watched with a pang of alarm.

"After Saturday night, I could wish him dead."

"Saturday night? I thought he was at the Heart Fund ball with Analisa?"

"That alone would have been sufficient," she snapped. "But I'm talking about afterward."

"As a matter of fact, love, I'm a little curious about that 'afterwards' myself. I knew he'd gone to see you. Tell me, what wild story did you offer him about how you learned of his trip to New York?"

"It was no wild story," Luisa said smugly. "I went to his office while he was out and saw the plane ticket lying on his desk."

Trenton laughed softly, a sinister sound that made the hairs rise on Analisa's arms. "Doll, you have just made my day." Quietly, he hung up.

Trenton walked into Roan's office, closed the door

behind him and leaned on it, searching Analisa's face with a wry smile, jiggling some coins in his trousers pockets. "Feel better?" Analisa nodded, tears suddenly sliding down her face. "Hey, you said you'd spent all those tears."

"Not the happy ones," she gulped, wiping at her face with the back of a hand. "I have buckets and buckets of happy tears, if I ever get the chance to use them. Trenton, he said he had no right to ask me to believe him. I thought it denoted g-guilt, I automatically c-condemned him."

"I think what it denoted was past guilt. *Would* you have believed him?" He moved across the room to sit on the corner of her desk, one leg dangling, one hand on the phone.

"I—needed to believe him."

"You're very much in love with him, aren't you, Analisa?" She nodded mutely. "And yet," he mused aloud, "despite the evidence, I think you've never been his mistress."

"No. I never have. I rejected him once in the beginning, because I was frightened. He's never . . . . wanted me since."

"Are you sorry you refused?" His voice, so wonderfully kind, was like an Open Sesame to her most secret thoughts.

"Yes. I'm sorry."

He sat gazing reflectively down at her. "Did it ever occur to you he might be saving you for something better than—a live-in job?"

She looked up at him hopefully. "What's he waiting for?"

"The right to your love. I gather he dug himself into a pretty deep hole before he woke up to the fact that holes are where the losers are buried." He picked up the phone and rang through to the sales-room on the intercom. "Harry, from now on there's a new policy. *No one,* and that includes Luisa Co-stenza, until rescinded by de la Corte, is to come into this office unescorted. Understood?"

When he'd concluded, the troubled look had re-turned to Analisa's eyes. "Trent, I asked Roan to take me with him."

"He couldn't. Analisa, believe me, it was not possi-ble."

"Why should it be impossible? Is he ashamed of me? Doesn't he trust me?" She wanted to believe in Roan, but she had been hurt too many times, and too many questions remained unanswered.

Trenton leaped up and began pacing the floor, run-ning one agitated hand through his wavy brown hair. "He just couldn't!"

"Trust me? Why not?" Her voice rose in distress.

"Do I have to spell it out for you?" he shouted. Sud-den terror chilled her through. Once before, Roan had prefaced a devastating warning with similar words. "Yes, I suppose I do." He resettled on the desk and lifted her chin solemnly. "Analisa, have you any idea what can happen to a man carrying half a mil-lion dollars in jewels?"

At closing time Analisa left the store by the front door accompanied by Harry, the head salesman. Trenton locked the door behind them from inside and returned to his workroom while Analisa re-mained a few minutes engaged in desultory conver-sation with the salesman, scarcely knowing what they discussed—for her heart and mind were too full of Roan. *Did Roan actually love her? Analisa de la Corte.* She couldn't help trying it on for fit. Perhaps if she showed him how deeply she reciprocated his love, she would have the supreme joy of spending the rest of her life with him, of bearing his name and his children!

Twilight was descending, bringing with it the usual winter evening chill; at this late hour few shoppers remained in the vicinity. Impatient to get away and eager to examine at leisure Trenton's revelation of Roan's love, Analisa bade good night to Harry and stepped from the curb. One moment the street had been empty of traffic, the next, out of nowhere, a car was careening drunkenly toward her.

"Miss Avalon!" Harry shouted, snatching her back from the hurtling black death, and she knew a thrust of fear as painful as impact. Was this what her mother had experienced in the final moments of her life? The driver's features had been shadowed by the oncoming darkness, but Analisa had seen the grim look on his face as he had fought to bring the wheel under control, passing within inches of where she had stood. It had been nothing more than a near accident, irrelevant to her father's destructive impulses or Trenton's disquieting revelation. She gasped for air like a near-drowned swimmer. Nearby a feminine voice shrilled, "Did you see that! He must be a sadist to pull a stunt like that. If she'd taken one more step—!" But Analisa put the implication of intent from her mind. It *had* been an accident: an ordinary black car, as unremarkable as that—or those—she'd noticed this morning. A coincidence, of course. Black cars were common. She ignored the voice in her head that said, "Not in Arizona."

Since Roan had given her the onyx desert rose bracelet, which she was rarely without, Analisa had developed a keen interest in sketching desert patterns which she felt could be worked into jewelry designs. She'd been too shy as yet to share any of her ideas with Roan, beyond the shoe clips she had suggested, but lately she had taken to spending long hours outdoors with a pen and sketch pad, enjoying her newfound artist's eye for line and color. She would make sketches of what she found and experiment with design possibilities as she went along. Wednesday morning she took her sketch pad to a favorite spot behind the house. Within a few weeks, California poppies and desert dandelions with blood-red hearts would be touching their golden fires to the hills; primrose would blossom white and pink against the winter-barren ground; phacelias would flaunt their purple scorpions' tails—a panorama she now anticipated eagerly. But winter too, offered its stark prizes of stately saguaro, comical cholla, and the arthritic-fingered green ephedra, that desert oddity that was sometimes brewed into a tonic known as Brigham or Mormon tea.

With her back braced against the citron trunk of a paloverde tree, she sat contemplating her many winter choices, wondering where to begin. She felt a sudden blast of wind like a tiny tornado whirling overhead and heard a *thonk!* Terrified, she realized an arrow was quivering not sixteen inches above her head, deeply imbedded in the paloverde trunk. A commotion among the tall sage and creosote bushes drew her attention to a burly figure, almost invisible in camouflaged clothing of spattered olives and browns, receding through the brush with a bow and full quiver of arrows.

Gathering her scattered supplies, she sped for home on quaking legs. Two accidents within a span of hours was more of a coincidence than she could bear to contemplate, although she knew she was being overdramatic simply because of Trenton's ominous warning.

CHAPTER 10

LATE THAT night two phone calls had summoned Analisa groping through the darkness to Roan's bedside phone. Both had been wrong numbers, but each time when she had hung up she had felt, in the silence of the darkened house, her heart thudding fearfully in her chest. She was long getting to sleep that night, but consciousness finally yielded to exhaustion. Sometime after midnight she was half-pulled from sleep by the renewed ringing of the phone. Another wrong number? It stopped in mid-ring and sleep quickly reclaimed her.

In the library, Roan dropped his light luggage to answer the phone before it could waken Analisa. He listened a moment, saying nothing, his face registering first surprise and then rage. When the caller hung up, he poured himself a stiff drink from the half-pint bottle in the bottom drawer of his desk. He stared at it with loathing a moment, then smashed the glass in the fireplace, splashing dark liquid inside the fire-blackened pit. In his own quarters he moved quietly in the darkness in order not to disturb the girl in the adjoining room. He showered, belted a robe about himself and went to stand beside Analisa's bed, staring at her for a long time. Then he went to his own bed, throwing off the warm robe and sliding naked beneath the covers.

Something woke Analisa and she lay motionless, listening, afraid even to open her eyes lest the fear in them give her away to the presence she sensed. The sound came again, a soft, protesting moan from the direction of Roan's empty room, and then anguished words. "No—no—*no!*" Her heart pounded with deep, heavy alarm. Roan was home, either hurt or caught in the grip of a ghastly nightmare. Leaping from her bed, she raced to his room. Roan was twisted in the covers of his bed. Moonlight touched his chest and face, highlighting his cheeks but shadowing his eyes so that at first she couldn't tell if they were open or closed. He moaned again, and his body jerked as if he flinched from pain.

"Roan," she whispered. "Roan, are you all right?" She touched his face and head lightly, testing for injury. He woke, recoiling from the unexpected touch. Then as his eyes focused on the girl bent over him in the moonlight, seeming as naked as a nymph in her diaphanous white gown, he reached up and pulled her to him.

"Analisa, you've come back," he breathed gratefully but senselessly, for it was he who had been away. He buried his face against her shoulder and with strong arms drew her to him. As he tucked her beneath the covers close beside him, she could have sworn she felt his tears against her throat.

She cradled his head, loving the feel of his black hair against her throat, his smooth cheek against her breast. "Roan, what is it, darling? What's troubling you? Are you hurt?"

He drew back his head to gaze into her concerned

eyes, as beckoning as the sea under moonlight. "You sent me away—bereft." He was slow in selecting the word. "I needed you then. I need you now. God, how I need you!"

She smiled. "I'm here, Roan," she whispered, running one hand across his cheek.

"You're beautiful, Analisa. Not just your face and your body, but all of you, in every way." As he spoke, he slowly moved one hand up to coax aside the flimsy strap of her gown. When Analisa made no motion to stop him, he moved in her arms, his lips claiming one hard, upthrust nipple. A murmur of exquisite delight broke from her lips, and Roan teased the hem of her long gown upward toward her waist.

"Oh, Roan," she moaned in a kind of desperate pleading. He rolled onto her, his lips seeking hers. Her mouth parted beneath his, eagerly, begging him to explore and taste and possess. She was begging, as he'd said she would, and it was the most wonderful thing she'd ever done. She moved beneath him, her hands stroking his body from the crown of his head to his rock-hard thighs, inviting him closer. There was a sudden instant of thrusting pain, tearing a strangled cry from her throat, and then unutterable, exultant joy.

She lay beside him and slept, and as she slept her hands sought the erotic places of his body that had been revealed to her. In her sleep she heard the pleasurable murmurings of his own sleep, and then simultaneously they woke, ignited again to their unquenchable need. This time her own tears—tears of joy—glistened against his throat.

Roan, first awake, stretched beside her propped on one elbow, suddenly threw the covers back so that he could enjoy a total, unobstructed view of Analisa's golden-white body. She woke slowly, smiling shyly at him, her eyes aglow. She had no idea when or how she'd shed her gown. She moved closer to Roan's warm body and gazed up at him lovingly.

"Analisa," he whispered, "why did you never tell me? Why did you let me think—?"

She pulled him down to bury her face against his chest, muffling her shy confession. "I've been half in love with you ever since I first saw you on my graduation night. Oh, Roan, if only you'd just taken me, instead of buying me. . . ." Her lips as she spoke brushed softly against his breast, and she was startled to feel the hardening of the flat male nipple. Intrigued, she experimentally touched it with the tip of her moist tongue. Flames leaped through her, momentarily paralyzing her with intense desire. Was this the way Roan's own body responded whenever his lips touched her? No wonder he had hated her when she'd rejected him! Far more than simply his ego had been at stake. Had he been burning with a need like this? Involuntarily, her arms slid about him, clinging fervently. "Roan, love me again. Prove to me it wasn't just some desperate, delightful dream—" His lips silenced her as his body obeyed.

He lay relaxed and contented on top of her, their limbs entwined. She knew she would never get enough of the feel of his skin against hers. Her arms tightened, and he lifted up onto his elbows, gazing down at her flushed face. "You're all woman, Analisa, as I promised you'd be . . ." There was laughter in his grey eyes, warm and soft. "I guess you know that I never meant for you to seduce me so easily."

"Easily!" she protested. "After these past four months, I'd never say you seduce easily!" Her own sparkling eyes, meeting his, became serious. "Roan,

I was terrified of falling in love with you and then losing you. By the time I realized how stupid I'd been to fight you and that I was already in love with you, it was too late. Oh, Roan, it's so easy to hurt the people who love you, and I've loved you so desperately—"

He kissed her tenderly. "Stay right where you are, darling. *I* am going to fix *you* breakfast in bed. Thank God it's Ardith's day off. We can spend the whole morning in bed."

He seemed to be gone a long time, but of course it was just that she was impatient for him to return—for the sight and touch and virile demands of his overwhelmingly male body. She propped herself on pillows, feeling exultant, wishing there was someone with whom she could share her happiness. Not Paris de la Corte—in unobtrusive ways, that woman had let it be known she didn't condone their living arrangement, but would welcome a marriage. She had refrained from direct criticism, since she could not condemn Analisa without also condemning her own son. The only other person was . . . Trenton. Why shouldn't Trenton be the first to know that one day soon she would be Mrs. Roan de la Corte? In a way, she owed her happiness to him—if it hadn't been for his revelation, she would never have felt so secure at last in Roan's love. . . .

She lifted the phone, but realized at once that it was in use. "That's my proposition, Mr. Rachmaninoff," she heard Roan say tautly. "Take it or leave it."

"I shall neither take it nor leave it, my boy." There was friendly exasperation in the unfamiliar voice that replied. "Had I preferred the money to the emerald, I should not have bought it in the first place. It is not for sale, and whatever your reasons for refusing to work on it, we both know it's nothing to do with your ability. Our contract is legal and binding and without an escape clause, and I've no intention of humoring you in this."

Analisa hung up very quietly, her fingers numb, unable to explain the terrible fear that gripped her. *Have you any idea what can happen to a man carrying half a million dollars in jewels?* Trenton had asked. Roan had in his possession a single emerald worth far in excess of that, a huge, perfect stone, recently found, for which she knew at least two men had already died. The famed, coveted Rachmaninoff Emerald.

Returning with breakfast, Roan was too preoccupied to notice Analisa's subdued mood. They sat side-by-side in bed, sipping coffee and sharing the eggs and toast Roan had assembled. When at last they set their trays aside, he tickled her nose and asked playfully, "And what kind of time did you have in my absence? If I have to go away again, will you welcome me home as sweetly?"

"Oh, don't go!" she cried earnestly, a tremor seizing her body. "I had a ghastly time without you." She told him about the careless driver who had nearly run her down, and about the arrow that had lodged inches above her head. "I guess it was a playboy who got his bunnies crossed," she quipped, but there was no answering humor in Roan's grim, calculating eyes. The shocked stillness of his face frightened her. The mood of the day had changed. By tacit consent they made no more love that morning; and shortly before noon he left for the Fifth Avenue shop.

She saw little of him in the days and evenings that

followed, though whenever they were together he treated her with affection. When she found herself deploring his absences, she reminded herself that he was making her birthday present. Yet never again did he invite her into his bed, and she was still too shy to press herself upon him. She often lay awake remembering how she had surrendered to temptation for one beautiful night and wishing Roan would come to her. Perhaps he was waiting until their wedding night. Their wedding night! Her heart leaped. When would that be? But Roan had never spoken of marriage. Could Trenton have been mistaken?

Late one evening she went to the front door in response to the playful chimes of the doorbell. "Darling, did you forget your—" she began as she flung the door open, and then stopped in dismayed consternation. "Trenton! Has something happened to Roan?"

"Of course not!" He stopped, looking discomfitted. "You mean he's not here? He left the office ahead of me, hours ago—"

"Oh! Trent, are you sure he's all right? I worry so about that filthy Rachmaninoff Emerald—"

"You know about that?" Abruptly he pushed past her through the door, slamming and locking it behind himself. "*No one* is supposed to know—"

"I overheard Roan talking to Mr. Rachmaninoff on the phone. Just a few accidental words—I wasn't eavesdropping. I've no idea what it was about, except that evidently Roan had changed his mind about wanting to work with it. I haven't mentioned it to anyone, not even to Roan. He's been working nights on it, I think—either on that or on the . . . the trinket for my birthday."

There was an odd expression on his honest brown face as he listened, half disbelief, half pity. He shook his head as if to clear his mind. "He hasn't begun to work on the emerald yet, though he may be creating the mounting for it. It's safely locked up in a vault somewhere. Not one of ours. Even I don't know where it is. When he starts work on the emerald itself, he'll be under armed guard every minute the stone is out of the safe."

"That's a relief, then. And what brings you here, Trenton?"

"I've come for the rest of my things. I've finally found a small apartment I can lease until the house is finished. It's looking like a June wedding."

She flitted about his room, chattering nervously about the wedding while Trenton gathered his few remaining possessions. She refused to think about his inadvertent disclosure that Roan had left work early. Trenton wasn't overly concerned for his safety, so why should she be?

When she followed Trenton back out of the bedroom, Roan was standing silently in the hall, grey eyes hostile as he watched her lithe figure, but it was to Trenton that he addressed himself. "Have you been making it a practice to drop in on my—*mistress*—these nights, Westfield?"

Analisa gasped, covering her flaming cheeks with her hands. Roan swung his attention immediately to her. "Is this why you've stayed out of my bed these past two weeks? Tell me, Analisa, does he satisfy you as much as I did?"

Trenton set aside his box of things and advanced on Roan murderously, fists doubled, and Analisa fully expected to see him flatten the taller man. Suddenly he seemed to deflate and stepped to one side.

No, they would not fight. Part of her was filled with disgust. Artists do not put their hands at risk, no matter what the provocation. But there was an unforgiving anger in Trenton's face, and she would not have been surprised to learn next day that he had terminated his apprenticeship to seek training and employment elsewhere.

No such thing happened. His name wasn't mentioned between them; very few words, in fact, passed between them on any subject. The freeze was on again, and Roan once more took to staying out nights. At times Analisa caught Roan staring at her with troubled eyes, almost as if he were beseeching her to unburden her guilt and beg his forgiveness. But she was guilty of nothing except loving him. He, on the other hand . . . how could he have said those things, even *thought* such things?

One morning Analisa was surprised to receive a luncheon invitation from Trenton. "No matter how strongly Roan feels about it, you've got to stop hiding and licking your wounds. You can't chain yourself for life to a stone pillar." She accepted reluctantly only after receiving adequate assurance that Trenton and Polly withheld no secrets from one another, and that Polly understood the situation.

It was not a comfortable luncheon. Trenton's eyes upon her were even more troubled than Roan's had been, though it may have seemed so only because Trenton made no attempt to hide his perturbation while Roan, as facile as a chameleon, would level her with a glittering look of scorn or animosity whenever he found himself observed.

"I'm surprised you're still working with Roan," she commented with forced levity.

"Ours is too compelling an association to dissolve

over personal issues. The truth is, and Roan recognizes it, that I may well have a talent equal to his own. My father was a significant craftsman in Florida. He never rose to such prominence as the de la Cortes, but that may be only because he could never afford Carlo Venturi for a teacher. Mine is a talent that I may well pass on to my children, particularly with Polly as their mother. She's a successful commercial artist in her own right, you know. And it looks like it's up to us, since Roan is too much the playboy—" He broke off abruptly, flushing with embarrassment.

"It's all right, Trent," she said quietly. "He's back with Luisa, isn't he? I've hardly deceived myself otherwise these past several days. And don't blame yourself. It started the very night after he—made love to me."

Trenton shook his head, and the tears prickling his eyes were almost her undoing. "Not particularly Luisa. It's a different one each night. The way he's playing the field, I doubt marriage will ever enter into his plans."

She gasped so painfully that he looked at her with freshly assessing eyes, and across the table his hands closed over hers. "Are you pregnant, Analisa?"

She shook her head wildly. "It's—it's too soon to tell, Trent. I don't think so. S-sometimes nerves can—create false clues. No, I'm surely not. Please, *please* don't say anything to Roan. If he comes to me, I want it to be as a husband and a lover, not as a father. If he married me only for—out of a sense of honor, not wanting me, we'd both be cheated."

"Your secret is safe with me, Analisa." There was sadness in his eyes.

They parted at her car, parked beside the store, after he'd persuaded her to go dancing with him on Saturday evening. "We'll call Polly before we leave if it'll ease your mind," he promised. "She knows what's happening between you and Roan, remember, and she's deeply concerned for you. She knows how Roan has isolated you—"

"But it's no concern of hers, and if I were her, I should hate your taking such personal responsibility for another woman."

"Analisa, I'd be a fool to think I could ever replace Roan in your life. Right?"

She smiled apologetically. "Right."

"Then understand this: In my life, there's no substitute for Polly Austen. Now, are you going to trust me?" She smiled gratefully and touched his arm, and as she did so a car door slammed violently beside them. She looked around directly into Roan's savage eyes, but he said nothing as he strode past them.

In the weeks that followed, Analisa plunged herself into her university studies with more determination than enthusiasm, reading every relevant book and article she could lay her hands on, submitting extra work to complement her required courses. Even so, without Trenton Westfield's attendance and unfaltering loyalty, she didn't think she could have made it through those denigrating weeks. Yet the day came when she saw their names linked in print on the society pages, and she knew it was time to give him back wholly to the understanding Polly Austen. When Analisa accepted what was to be his final luncheon invitation, it was for the purpose of writing *finis* to his championship, though she hoped it would not mean the end of their friendship.

The restaurant was crowded, noisy enough for her

to speak frankly without attracting attention, but before she could broach the subject, Roan stalked up to their table, his eyes blazing with fury.

"I think, Analisa, this has gone far enough." He spoke quietly, but his resonant voice carried through the entire room, which had suddenly gone avidly still. "I have remained silent as long as you confined your activities to your respective bedrooms, but I'll not tolerate this blatant public display of lust. I've got what I wanted from you: one night in your bed, and now you can consider your debt paid!"

Analisa stared at him, white-faced and horrified as the pain of his cruel public denouncement cut through every raw fiber of her being. Fury and shame and despair overcame her better judgment. "Three times, Roan—what does that figure out to? About sixteen-thousand dollars a—a—*performance?* I expect I shall go down in the *Guinness Book of World Records* as—as—t-the most expensive w-whore in history. But which one of us will go down as the biggest fool?"

Trenton brought his fist down furiously on the table, smashing dishes. "*Shut up,* both of you!" He turned to his associate. "Good God, Roan, do you have to rub her nose in her father's dirt?"

Analisa leaped from the table to make her escape, but Roan caught her wrist. "I'm not through, Analisa. Hear me out clearly. I don't want you back in my house. Not for any reason, not for one minute. I'll have your clothes sent over to your lover's apartment tomorrow." His eyes raked her insolently. "That should be soon enough. You won't need anything for tonight. We both know how you sleep, don't we?"

* * *

When Trenton had left her alone in his rooms, she paced the floor like a maddened animal. She had no idea where this apartment was. He had driven her here in grim silence in her own car and had then returned to work in a cab. Suddenly she stopped pacing. She pressed her stomach, feeling hysterical. Fifteen days late—was she pregnant? How could she bear to have the child of a man who had abused her so cruelly, a child born of travesty and not of love? There were places in California where she'd be handled with expediency and anonymity. . . .

After fleeing Trenton's apartment it had taken her several minutes to orient herself and make her way home. Home? Never again. She flung clothes into her suitcases and packed as many of her things as she could fit into the trunk and rear seat of her coupe, for she'd not be coming this way again. She laid the ebony and desert rose bracelet on the vanity. She wanted no reminders of Roan. Nothing. In a few days, she would unburden herself of the most potent reminder of all, the one she carried beneath her heart, the one she had once wanted with such longing.

She went to the Carefree branch bank where Roan had opened an account for her and transferred all the money into traveler's checks. Until now she had refused to touch his generous allowance, but now he must pay for the expulsion of his seed from her body, and help her reestablish herself in a respectable job in a sane world.

Driving away from the bank, she noticed a yellow car behind her, the driver's face partially concealed by a hat pulled low over his brow. It was still behind her when she turned through Paradise Valley on Lincoln Drive, and when she drew up before the familiar house on Camelback Mountain. She would say good-bye to her father, and then she would disappear forever. But the house was shuttered and bleak, a For Sale sign posted at the wrought iron gate. She turned despondently away. Where was her father? What was he thinking, doing? Would word of Roan's denouncement of her filter back to him? Swinging from the empty driveway, she saw again the yellow car, and filled with rage that Roan should have her followed, spied upon, she drove like a lunatic down the winding streets of the mountain, entering rush hour traffic at high speed, twisting and turning down unexpected streets, jumping lights wherever intersections were clear, until she was satisfied she had lost her pursuer.

Then she drove slowly west out of the city. Before long, night came, and every sweep of headlights coming up behind her was like the devil surfacing from a black hole in hell to pursue her. When her nerves could stand no more, she found a run-down but clean motel off the main highway and crawled inside to lick her wounds.

She made a late start next day because she'd been too sick to leave her bed. Setting out in the early afternoon, she followed roads at random so long as they led generally north and west. At some small town, she would stop to inquire of a Planned Parenthood unit where she could get an abortion. But she was too sick, physically and emotionally, to face anyone yet. Her hands clenched tightly to the wheel, her stomach tight with pain, she kept on driving, aimlessly choosing her roads, stopping only for gas and restrooms, not bothering to eat. "You could have my baby, Analisa," Roan had said. No, she couldn't! She would kill his baby, while it was still so small and shapeless she could think of it as an act of cleansing, and not an act of murder. God, how she wanted his baby! Hot blinding tears poured down her cheeks and splashed like acid onto her hands.

The road wound upward, narrowing, pavement spottily yielding to gravel. The air grew cooler as night fell. Clouds advanced in the dark sky, and rain fell lightly. Springtime on the balmy desert was a wintry March storm on the mountaintop. She turned on the heater and kept going, heedless of the first sleety snow that drove at her windshield like shot fired from a black-muzzled cannon.

The cold wind subsided, and the snow drifted thicker and softer as she climbed, swirling about her, weighting down the windshield wipers, accumulating on the road that by now had become no more than a narrow track. She had the sensation of driving between walls of trees, though she could see nothing beyond the revolving black-and-white barrel which the world had become, making her feel so dizzy that she gripped the wheel tighter.

She was not used to winter driving conditions, and her car was not equipped for them. Whatever signposts might have guided her were buried under wet, clinging snow. She ought to go back. But the road was now too narrow to risk turning. If only she would reach the summit and start down the other side! She seemed to have been climbing straight up forever.

The car slid sickeningly, and she wrenched the wheel in panic, sliding to a halt against an unpainted wooden fence, its irregular grey boards gaping through the fallen snow like decaying teeth. Three of the teeth collapsed beneath the impact of her bumper, and hanging askew in the beam of her headlights, knocked free of the wetly plastering snow, was a rusting, rifle-shot metal rectangle warning, "No Trespassing." Did that mean, then, she was Somewhere? Or only that she might have been, had she arrived years earlier? Could someone here point her the way back to the highway?

Switching off the headlamps and taking a flashlight from the glove compartment, she got out and walked along the tumbled wooden barrier in search of a gate, her feet rapidly becoming numb with wet and cold. Her fingers, outstretched to help guide her through the snow and darkness, closed around a wire loop. Working clumsily in the failing light of her torch, she freed the loop, the rancher's time-honored gate latch, from its wooden anchor and with all her strength pushed the leaning gate against the drifted snow behind it. In vain she flashed the weak beam ahead in search of a building, some sign of human habitation here at the end of the world. As she stepped through the gate her feet tangled in a strand of wire stretched low across the ground, sending the flashlight flying from her hand and into a snowbank. Her last conscious impression as she fell forward into the downy oblivion of the snow was of a great clattering of bells and gongs shattering the deadly still of night.

CHAPTER 11

O N the mountaintop, fall came early. Huddled on a hard pallet on the bare floor of a one-room hut, shielded from the family who lived there by a single dingy sheet suspended from the ceiling, Analisa lost the spring and the summer. From time to time, gypsy-bright figures darted around her like hummingbirds, seen yet not seen, heard and yet not quite heard, their faces and unintelligible voices as gentle as their clothes were colorful. "Don't let them find me! The yellow car . . ." she had pleaded as wiry arms had lifted her from the snow and carried her into the lantern-lit shack. The yellow car—Analisa's memory began and ended there. She had delivered herself into the care of this strange-tongued family, a man and two women, and though they had understood scarcely a word she'd said, they had read well her crippling fear.

After much hand-wringing and soul-searching, *la madre vieja*, the old woman who was the short, wiry man's mother, had ordered the car brought inside the rotting fence and stored in the dilapidated out-building that housed the puny goat that would give milk for the *niño* coming to them in the summer, and the scrawny chickens that gave eggs and meat to the young wife who was bulging with child.

Of the three—the tired mother-to-be, the wrinkled *suegra* and the kelp-haired, mustachioed small-statured husband/son/father-to-be—only the latter seemed to resent the intrusion. Manuel Vasquez was not a cruel man, or even unkind. But he was a hunted man. A year ago he had led his mother and his young wife, then so pretty and dainty, now almost as used-up looking as her old *suegra*, barefoot across the Rio Grande at El Paso, where the waters were ankle-deep and too rambling to be guarded every minute at every point. Bringing only what they could carry on their backs, they crossed the river hours—or perhaps only minutes—ahead of a posse who sought Manuel for an outrage he couldn't prove he hadn't committed. For weeks he had scrabbled out a living for his beloved and ever-hungry women, working for starvation wages for dirt farmers who were little better off than he, afraid to apply for the precious green card that made the difference between pennies and migrant farmers' union wages, that magic *tarjeta* that would erase the status of Unemployable Illegal Mexican Alien, that treacherous little card that could identify and send him back to Chihuahua and the unforgiving Mexican law. *La pequeña tarjeta verde* that was a kind of cruel American god.

Week after week they had drifted across the forbidding deserts of New Mexico and Arizona and on into California, working at sundry menial, underpaid tasks. Eventually they'd made their way northward into the San Jacinto Mountains where a high-country small rancher, with no questions asked, had given them refuge—an ill-paying job and this broken-down one-room shanty with its drafty walls, leaking roof and bare-board floors, its shattered panes and pot-bellied stove that roasted anyone within five feet of it and left all those beyond its unsympathetic perimeters to freeze. It was not the American Dream, but it was cleaner and less inhospitable than a Mexican jail, and they were together.

They could not surrender the copper-haired girl to the authorities without jeopardizing their own precious anonymity. Neither could they leave her to die in the snow. To summon a doctor was equally impossible. In the weeks that followed, the two women virtually prayed her to stay alive in vivid and earnest language of which Analisa could not have understood more than a word here and there even had she not been in a moribund state. Each day Manuel would ride off on the ranch-provided brown mare to tend his employer's fences and irrigation ditches and winter-hungry cattle.

They had examined Analisa's wallet for identification, gasped at the fortune in traveler's checks, dreamed of the warm clothes and bedding and food such wealth could provide, and then tucked it carefully beneath the straw of her bed. They dared not touch it. They dared not do anything at all to call attention to themselves. They lived in daily fear, never asking themselves, "Is this really freedom?" just enduring. The women never ventured farther from the shack than necessary to gather firewood, to tend the animals and garden, or to wash their pitiful clothes at the stream beyond the gate where every day Manuel checked the wire-trap over which Analisa had stumbled, setting into motion the hanging, clattering conglomeration of scrap metal that served as an alarm.

Weeks passed and no one sought the girl. Manuel, whose stomach was gnawed into burning holes with a lifetime of hunger, convinced himself it would be right and safe to take reimbursement for the fervent care with which his women tended the stranger who lay on the mat in the corner. Piece by piece he began to dismantle the beautiful car, stowing the parts in his saddlebags, riding once a week down the mountainside to sell them for a fraction of their value to a Spanish-speaking accomplice, growing bolder with each illicitly disposed-of article that stirred no reprisal from the world where the girl obviously belonged. At first the women had used the beautiful fur jacket to cover the girl, but as the weather warmed, that, too, went to the accomplice in the valley and with it the few pieces of jewelry Manuel had rummaged surreptitiously from Analisa's cases while the women were elsewhere occupied.

Throughout the months of spring and summer, only the half-heard prayers of the two women sustained Analisa. In the first days of fall, she heard the whimpers and screams of childbirth, then the squalling of a newborn baby—angry, frightened, defiant infant howls—and she left her bed for the first time, pulled from it as if by some eccentric force, as disoriented as a sleepwalker. Her copper-gold hair had grown almost to her waist, her sea-green eyes emitted pain and admitted nothing; her sweetly curved cheekbones were made prominent by her thin cheeks. She was a slender, beautiful, empty vase waiting to be filled with the ingredients of life. Now at last she could bathe and dress and feed herself. She helped, automatonlike, around the premises.

She cradled the newborn baby in her arms and was glad that he at least, in contrast to the ragged garments and meager fare of the adults, had pretty clothes and a few toys and plenty of formula. Still not one word had passed her lips, not one tear had left her eyes since that night she had said, "Don't let them find me! The yellow car . . ."

One copper-bright evening she stood gazing out past the ruined fence and a memory stirred, then collapsed, leaving her with her first faint curiosity about the world beyond the sagging gate. Red-leaved vines mingled with the gold of quaking aspen, and beyond and above them rose the rose-trunked ponderosas. She reached out, as a baby might reach for a mobile suspended above its crib, and pushed open the broken gate, unconsciously stepping carefully over the wire snare that had sent her tumbling—when? There had been snow on the ground, the deep of winter, and now the leaves were turning . . .

In the woods she sat motionless on a dry rock in the middle of a tumbling stream, mesmerized by the chiaroscuro waters. The laughter of the water as it leapt from stone to stone was tranquilizing, reminding her dimly of some forgotten happiness, the sound of a mill wheel turning in its stream, a waterfall splashing beside a lover's bed . . . It covered the stealth of approaching footsteps, and not until she heard the sharp twang of a bowstring did she look up to see a man on the far side of the stream, half invisible in paislied olive and brown camouflage, bow arm still outstretched as if to ram the arrow to its target. With a cry of panic, the first sound to leave her lips in six months, she leaped to her feet. The hunter turned sharply, exclaiming in surprised apology, but the sound of his voice asking her to "Wait!" only lent lightning to her feet thundering across the leaf-moulded turf.

They were all there, the memories savaging her mind. Roan, who had loved and then hated her . . . her tragic, ruined father. . .the irresponsible bowhunter on the hill . . . the black car that had nearly struck her and the yellow car that had pursued her . . . and the baby. . . . Somewhere she had heard a baby crying, and it was hers, *hers.* Roan's baby. But what had happened to the weeks—the months?—between the yellow car and the crying baby?

She burst into the shack, clear eyes revealing a cleared mind. She stared at her rescuers in bewildered astonishment. The hummingbird women, the acrid-smelling man. . .they had been there scything in and out of her long, long dream.

"My baby," she pleaded at last. "Where is my baby?" The trio stared at her, amazed but uncomprehending. She locked her fingers together to make a cradling motion with her arms.

"Bebé?" The wrinkled old crone exchanged glances with her daughter-in-law. *"Usted—no tiene bebé."*

"But there is! I've heard him cry! I've held him in my arms. I remember . . ." She furrowed her brow, trying to recall what little Spanish she had learned from the Mexican workers at her father's restaurants. *"Preñada."* She clasped one hand to her stomach. *"Estaba preñada. Oi llorar a mi niño."*

"No! No! Mi bebé!" The younger woman rushed to the curtained corner and returned clutching her baby fearfully to her breast, expostulating volubly. *"Mi bebé. Los ojos de su papá."*

Analisa stared at the black eyes and hair of the brown-skinned infant. "But—*mi bebé—dónde?*"

The women, watching her sadly, did not respond. Manuel, grimy and foul-smelling from his day on the hot, windy *sierra*, watching the charade between the women in uneasy silence, now moved defensively close to his frightened wife, his black hair and eyes echoed in the small face of his tiny son. "You go," he said bluntly with an almost incomprehensible accent. "You not need now." It was the first time she'd heard him speak English, though she'd often heard his voice in her long dream. "Your *bebito* . . . lost. This our *bebito*. Son of Manuel and Ester—" He stopped abruptly, the wariness in his eyes blocking out all other emotions. Rapidly he concluded, "*El nieto de mi madre.* All God has left us. You not take."

His only child. His mother's grandson. And her own baby . . . her terror and her accident had cost her that. Was this the terrible price she paid for once wishing herself free of Roan's precious seed?

"*Sí.* I go. *Mañana,*" she agreed. To emphasize her meaning, she began frantically pushing her jumbled clothing into the only suitcase in evidence. She assumed the other cases were still in the car—wherever that was. She paused to look up at her benefactors. "My car. Where is it?" The man had taken himself off to wash at the stream beyond the crumbling fence, and the women feigned incomprehension, or truly did not understand. She groped for the Spanish words. "*Mi automóvil. Dónde está?*" The younger woman began to point excitedly toward the sagging outbuilding where Analisa had seen the goat and the pitiable chickens; and the old *abuela,* grinning with dawning comprehension, brought Analisa's wallet out from its hiding place.

Upon finding the skeletal remains of her once-beautiful Continental coupe, Analisa was first appalled and then furious. Halfway back to the shack, she met Manuel returning from his evening ablutions at the stream. If she hadn't been so enraged, she would have been amused to see with how little difficulty the man now understood every word of her English.

Manuel heard her out, his hands riding nonchalantly on frayed pocket edges. When she was quiet, he shrugged indifferently, yet with a suggestion of arrogance. "We feed you. Months. We—*mi madre* give you bed, be your *cura—mi esposa fué su médico*—your doctor. You owe. We sell car—*poco a poco*—"

"I have money. I would have paid you—"

"*Cuándo?* When? You know nothing, do nothing, like sleeping bear in winter."

"I'll pay you now."

"Checks! Checks no good. We take cash already. We sell clothes. We eat *todos los días*—every day. *Bebito* hungry all time. *Mi madre y mi esposa siempre tienen hambre,* hungry." He clutched at his own rumbling, burning stomach, and the real pain he felt there pierced his brilliant, defiant eyes.

Analisa gasped. There was a kind of logic to the man's claim. He could have left her to die in the snow—indeed, had she not caught her foot in the snare she probably would have died. It took little imagination to understand why this pitiful little refugee family needed such a warning device. Yet whatever their own pursuing demons, they had shared their home with the stranger who had been thrust upon them, the women tending her with the same devotion they might have given one of their own.

She had no idea what day it was, even what month, only that the mountaintop had donned fall colors and she had come here very early in the spring, before winter's grip had been broken. She had been trying not to think about the days preceding her accident. A kind of nausea began to creep up from the depths of her soul as the full and terrible and inescapable memories returned. With a shock, she recalled the For Sale sign that had left her utterly homeless and hopeless on that traumatic day late in March and she wanted with all her heart to see her weak, beloved, ineffectual father again, to talk to him, gladly forgiving the unforseeable consequences of his moral and emotional illness. As for Roan, whose betrayal had been deliberate and malicious, whose baby she no longer carried—she would not think of him again. All her sad, lost, frightened feelings touched her wide-eyed face as the memories crowded in on her in an overwhelming rush. For the first time, it occurred to the man that to be American and wealthy, young and beautiful, did not guarantee happiness, and he felt shame for what he had done.

"How am I to leave here?" she asked, rousing herself to the present.

"*Mi amigo*—he come tomorrow—day after. Bring you to town. You take bus, go. Never come back.

"I'll send you some money for your kindness—"

"No!" Sharp as gunshot. "You not write, not remember. We—*no existimos. Comprendes?*"

It was two days before anyone came for Analisa, during which she helped willingly with the household chores, harvesting apples from a stunted tree in a corner of the yard, salvaging the last of the tomatoes and squash in the frost-nipped garden. She especially loved holding and tending the dark-eyed baby boy. With sign language and their few common words, the women were able to communicate sufficiently. Manuel, returning from work, would wash and shave at the mountain stream, which seemed to grow icier with each passing fall day. Afterward he would sit passively in a corner of the room, fear and impatience burning in his eyes. By now, Analisa knew for certain that he had taken every cent of her ready cash—not a lot, for most of it had been in traveler's checks—as well as her mink jacket, her jewelry, and most of her clothes. The loss did not disturb her so much as the thought that Manuel had been able to dispose of stolen goods without seemingly so much as a ripple of concern from those who should have noted her long absence.

She didn't like the way Manuel's *amigo* leered when he came to take her off the mountain. The women helped her to load her things into the battered old Ford with its mangled fenders and smashed headlight, the rear bumper tied on with fencing wire and a windowless rear door wired closed. This *amigo* was no doubt the contact who had received Manuel's stolen goods. Traveling down the mountain road at breakneck speed—probably more the result of faulty brakes than of power in the engine—she made no protest; she couldn't be free of her chauffeur soon enough. She wondered if he spoke any English, but didn't test him and was not enlightened until they reached the foot of the mountain and drifted into the narrow, chuck-holed streets of a village of which Analisa had no recollection.

"Manuel's in big trouble over the border. He could use a little payment for his help. I can see he gets the money if you'd like to leave a couple hundred with me." He spoke with no trace of accent, and his slyness made Analisa's skin crawl.

"He's already been paid," she said icily. "And I rather imagine you've collected a good share yourself. Nevertheless, if you'll stop by a bank, I'll cash a check and pay you for bringing me down. Then if you'd drop me at the bus depot—"

At the bank her driver held out an eager hand as she dropped four five-dollar bills into his palm. He continued to hold it there with greedy expectancy. "That probably figures about a dollar a mile round trip," she told him sharply.

He licked his lips. "Sure you wouldn't like to change your mind about a little something for Manuel?"

"I'm sure. Now if you'd drop my things over there—" She waved in the direction of the bus station, a quarter block away. "However," she added thoughtfully. "I'd like to send a gift to Ester and the old *abuela*. How should I address it?"

He shrugged rudely. "Who knows? A man running from the law of two countries doesn't exactly advertise his home address." He pulled up before the little-and-ill-used looking bus terminal. Slouching indolently behind the wheel of the car he waited while Analisa carried her own luggage, just as it had been up to the women to load for the journey down. As she removed the last item, he departed with a roar and a clatter that almost threw her off balance.

She stood staring at the bus schedule posted on the wall, scarcely seeing it. She wanted desperately to see her father. Whatever the hazards, wherever he

might be, she needed to know that he was all right.
Perhaps he could join her, away from the influence of
the Costenza family and whatever other gaming organizations flourished on the blood and souls of the
weak—where Roan de la Corte could never again
hurt and humiliate her. She was shocked to see by
the daily calendar on the wall that it was already
nearly mid-October. More than six months of her life
had been spent in an oblivion too deep for even night-
mares to penetrate.

She got some change from the station attendant
and went to the pay phone to dial the number of the
only restaurant her father still retained. An unfamiliar voice answered, and she asked cautiously for
"Orlando." There was a moment of silence.

"Orlando?" asked the bewildered voice.

"Orlando Avalon. This *is* the Old Mill Restaurant,
isn't it?"

"Oh! Oh, yes. But it's no longer the property of the
Avalons. Orlando Avalon died several months ago."

Analisa suppressed a cry and gripped the receiver.
"Died? Died—how? When?"

"A heart attack. While he was driving. It was in
April, I think, maybe early May, not long after the
restaurant changed hands. Who did you say was calling?"

Very quietly, as if sneaking out a back door to
avoid an unpleasant confrontation, Analisa depressed the disconnector with one fingertip before
dropping the receiver back into place. So this was
why she had been able to drop so completely out of
sight. Her father was dead, and Roan didn't care.
But it hurt that not even Trenton Westfield, the only
kind person who had walked her lonely path with
her, had sought her. The room seemed to be dark-

ening and revolving around her. Oblivion beckoned. . . .

She looked up to see Manuel's *amigo* leering at her
through the grimy plate-glass window, and she lifted
her chin. Somewhere there was healing work to be
done. Someone needed her help and compassion, just
as she had needed the love and care of the Mexican
women. No one—no man, no organization—was ever
again going to come close to destroying her.

She marched to the counter and bought a ticket to
the first city that popped into her head.

CHAPTER 12

In San Francisco she worked as relief cook in a chain restaurant to support herself through airline flight attendant school. When she joined the airline, it was with the understanding she would not make Phoenix runs. On those occasions when she was so scheduled, another stewardess was always willing to trade.

She volunteered her services at a school for emotionally disturbed children and at a retirement home. She sketched and took piano lessons and wandered for hours along the beaches, listening to the anesthetizing drum of surf upon sand. She lived alone, rarely entertained and never dated, though there was ample opportunity. Her pain was a private thing, too cruel to hide and too deep to share. She had lost her home, her parents, her lover, her baby; she had been pursued by demons in camouflage clothing and in black cars and in yellow ones; but worst of all, she had lost her identity and her integrity when Roan de la Corte had lifted her to heaven only to hurl her into the depths of hell. She had lost her self-esteem when she had allowed him to do it. She sought absolution in service; the world forgave, if indeed there was anything to forgive, but she couldn't forgive herself. She held herself aloof, to the bafflement of her costewardesses and to the dismay of hopeful pilots, of ground crewmen and reservations officers and commissary personnel. "Half a pair of scissors isn't much good," one of the pilots coaxed. "Together we could really cut up." She smiled—that sweet, wistful smile that never touched her troubled eyes—and thanked him, and went her own way, as always, alone.

She was compellingly aware of the man in first class who studied her with almost critical professionalism, his amber eyes revealing nothing of his conclusions. His medium-length blond hair was silvered at the temples, from sun or from worry, but not, she thought, from age. His full lips were gentle, and his benign face was etched with lines that spoke of cares conquered. Though he was not exceptionally tall—a little under six feet, she thought as she left the plane in the company of the copilot and another stewardess—he stood out in the crowd that surrounded the exit ramp, awaiting arrivals. He waited for her. "Why do I get the impression I've seen you before?" he asked, but there was none of the brashness she'd come to expect in this overworked approach.

The copilot at her side squeezed her arm. "Remember," he chided softly in her ear, "I was in line way ahead of him."

She smiled almost apologetically and turned back to the stranger. She knew who he was, just as she knew who all the passengers were. Barry Marcus. The light jacket over his suntanned arm, hiding the brown leather briefcase, told her his flight had originated in a cooler climate. "Do you fly with us often,

Mr. Marcus?" she asked, noting that he was pleased, but not flattered, to be identified.

"Occasionally. Three times a year, perhaps."

"Then that must account for it. I've been on board for six months—we've probably shared a flight in the past."

He smiled engagingly. "Then you must have been wearing a gunnysack over your head. Anything that recent I'd not have forgotten. No, I think it goes back much farther than that."

Immediately the expression changed in her tragic green eyes. "Surely not," she said tersely and turned abruptly from him.

His hand descended on her arm, compelling but not commanding. "Please wait, Analisa. This is not your ordinary pickup."

She looked up at him with a bittersweet smile. "Are they ever?"

He grinned and fell into step beside her, his hand still in possession of her arm. "Never, I'm sure. Have a cup of coffee with me? Talk to me a few minutes. You look lonely. I'm lonely."

There was a calmness about him, an air of hard-acquired serenity that spoke of great strength. She nodded, having intending to visit the coffee shop anyway before going home to the immaculate, sterile apartment that she shared only with the ghosts that would not be forgotten.

"Analisa what?" he asked, stirring his coffee and eyeing the name badge pinned to her smartly tailored jacket. He smiled disarmingly.

"Avalon."

"You have a beautiful, expressive face," he said warmly. She waited impatiently for him to move on to the desirability of her body. Then she would walk away from him without a backward glance. "It will never stop haunting me until I've captured it on film."

Beneath the table she crushed her napkin in her fist. "I'm afraid that will be impossible, Mr. Marcus. I never pose for photographers. I presume you are Marcus of *Images of Marcus,* the apotheosis of every model's hopes."

"I could do great things for you, Analisa. I can make you famous. I can make you rich."

"I was rich once, Mr. Marcus." For the first time there was a steely ring in her voice. "It shouldn't happen to the devil himself."

His eyes narrowed as he fumbled in his discarded jacket, producing a crumpled pack of cigarettes. "Do you mind?" She shook her head, and he struck a chrome lighter to the cigarette between his lips. "Obviously you don't smoke. You smell too sweet and your teeth are too white. I think," he added sternly, "if I ever caught you smoking, I'd turn you over my knee and make the other end smoke."

A small light exploded in her heart. It was as if he cared a little bit. Only her parents—and perhaps Trenton Westfield, a little—had ever cared about her. "I won't model for you, Mr. Marcus." she said dryly, reverting to an earlier topic, not wanting to dwell on those other thoughts. He mustn't care; no one must ever care again, for she had nothing to give in return.

"Barry," he corrected firmly. "So you won't model for me. For now, I'll accept that, though I don't promise not to try again. So we'll just be friends."

"I'm afraid that will be impos—"

He silenced her with an upraised hand. "Hear me out, Analisa. A man would have to be blind not to see the hurt that's been inflicted upon you—and dense, not to guess its source. You think you can never love again, and you may be right. To some, love only comes once, deeply. If you also are one who believes that platonic friendship cannot exist between a man and a woman, then I must tell you now that ours will be a dead-end relationship." He drew deeply on his cigarette and exhaled smoke, obscuring his own eyes as he studied the reaction in hers. "I'm married, Analisa. My wife and I have been separated for five years, but there will be no divorce. We're Catholic. My religion, which means a great deal to me, forbids remarriage, as well as adultery. Friendship, Analisa Avalon. That's all I can or ever will offer you."

Her lips trembled. "Thank you, Barry Marcus. I should be pleased to accept your offer."

They spent a lot of time together walking or picnicking on the beach, occasionally but not often holding hands; dining out elegantly or dining in casually at home—his apartment or hers; listening to records; reading together; attending concerts and symphonies or the ballet, or frolicking through Golden Gate Park. Analisa once asked him why they never went dancing, and he'd said simply, "I'm human, Analisa. To hold you in my arms . . ."

She remembered Roan's arms about her and shivered with longing. "I can do without dancing, Barry."

Neither ever breached the other's privacy, though once he asked her, "What do you do for joy in your life?"

"Joy? There is no joy. I work to feed my stomach and keep my brain alive; I serve to keep my heart alive. My cup runneth not over, but it's sufficient."

They were as comfortable together as an old shoe

and a sock, because neither ever made demands upon the other. It didn't occur to them that in their care not to intrude they were in fact too reticent with each other.

"Do you have children?" Analisa asked dreamily one afternoon, sitting on the beach with her cheek resting on her upraised knees.

There was a telling silence, and with a sudden movement he tossed his half-smoked cigarette into the surf where its dying hiss was lost beneath the crash of an incoming wave. "I have a daughter. I *had* a daughter!"

She held her breath, then asked, "Won't your wife let you see her?"

He looked at her with stormy, bitter eyes. "She couldn't care less. I visit Beth whenever I can get to LA, maybe twice a month. The doctors don't approve—they say I leave her depressed—but I see her anyway. God! She has to have someone!"

Analisa felt the pain in his eyes and voice. "Tell me about her, Barry."

"There's little to tell. She was a normal, happy, healthy child in every way until she was seven; a model, uncomplicated daughter when I left for a trip to Phoenix six years ago to set up a branch studio. When I returned two weeks later, she was silent and vicious except for fitful, unintelligible screaming. With me, she was merely sullen, but she would attack her mother savagely, without apparent provocation. We tried to cope at home, but eventually we had to place her in a hospital for disturbed children. By then, it was too late for our marriage. Instead of drawing us together, as such an experience should have done, it split us apart. Doria decided to go her own way. She continued to visit Beth until the doctor recommended that she stay away, on the grounds that her visits excited—*incited* was his indiscreet word—Beth to violence. Doria was almost eager, I think, to be shed of the responsibility. I haven't seen Doria in over four years. I've heard she's living with someone in Indiana—a fellow she used to know here. A fellow whom, I suspect, she'd been seeing regularly behind my back. Beth does seem calmer now, but—"

"—But she never forgives."

Analisa wasn't aware she'd spoken her thoughts aloud until her companion exclaimed sharply, "Forgives? What an odd thing to say!"

"Something traumatic must have happened to her during those two weeks you were away. People don't just suddenly regress without some reason, and surely if it had been a congenital problem it would have manifested itself long before age seven. I assume you did have her examined for any physical injury?"

"Eventually. At first, my wife absolutely refused. She insisted there could have been no accident, no injury, without her knowledge. She had always been a good mother—she didn't let Beth run around unsupervised. As it turned out, the neurologists and brain specialists found nothing."

"On my next flight to Los Angeles, may I go see her, Barry?"

He doubted the wisdom of that, but consented to her accompanying him as an unseen observer. On her second trip she obtained Barry's reluctant permission to visit his daughter. She found the girl hostile and uncommunicative. She also found that the child's doctor and all her attendants were women— she would not suffer any male attendants near her.

172

Only her father's attentions did not throw her into hysteria, so long as he made no move to embrace her; conversely, she sank into deep apathy for days after seeing him. Analisa had looked into the child's brown eyes and seen her own green ones staring back at her. She knew her instinct was correct: the child had been brutally hurt. She kept mulling over every word Barry had told her, and when she returned to San Francisco she asked him to have his daughter transferred to the school for disturbed children where she volunteered her services. "So I can see her more often. Gain her confidence. Love her. Oh, Barry, I need someone to love!"

Early in August Beth Marcus was transferred to the Bay Area School, where both her father and Analisa became frequent visitors, though not, at Analisa's urging, simultaneously. There was no miraculous improvement in the girl's condition, but her teacher confided, after a few months, that she no longer withdrew into herself after each paternal visit. "I believe you were right. The child needed more, not less, of her father's attention. He's still the only man who can get near her, though."

Beth was considerably less hostile toward Analisa, too. "I wish I could accomplish for her what Ester and her old *suegra* accomplished for me," Analisa mused aloud one evening as she sat on the floor at Barry's feet. She had not thought of her benefactors in weeks, though in the first months after her departure her inability to do anything at all for them had haunted her. "If I could work the miracle for Beth that they worked for me—".

Barry kneeled before her, taking her face between his hands, his amber eyes probing deep into hers. "What miracle, Analisa? Who is Ester? I will send my daughter anywhere, to anyone who can send her back to me whole."

Analisa shook her head regretfully. "I owe my life to two Mexican women, yet I don't even know who or where they are. They live somewhere on a mountaintop in the San Jacinto Range, near a little town whose name I don't even recall. They had no medical knowledge and neither the means nor the courage to summon a doctor because—for some reason I never learned—they were outside the law. They couldn't speak English, and they hadn't even enough food for themselves. But they cared for me, kept me clean and fed, and prayed for me, asking nothing in return. I don't know how it worked, I only know it did." She stared sadly into a time and place Barry couldn't see. "If it were in my power, I'd give them the right to live free and unafraid again. And yet I can give them nothing. I can only repay my debt to them by helping someone else."

Barry's hand caressed her cheek, his eyes compassionate, "Tell me, Analisa. Tell me about this terrible thing that happened to you and how these people might help my daughter."

"I was ill and unconscious. They could so easily have turned their backs on me, but instead they turned their faces to God and prayed for someone called Analisa, and the warmth and love that seeped into me told me that I was Analisa. What little they had, they shared with me freely, and it was enough— because I knew that someone, somewhere, cared." Someone, but not Roan. She pushed the thought roughly away. "Suddenly one day I was aware again, remembering, and their selflessness is what gave me the strength and courage to make my own way alone." He gathered her in his arms for the first time and felt the shaking of her body and wondered why she didn't release the tears she so clearly needed to cry. It was the closest intimacy they'd ever shared, and soon Analisa removed herself from his arms.

"I know it's unorthodox," she confessed, "and I suppose the teachers would be appalled if they knew, but every day before I leave Beth I kneel at her bed with her and I pray aloud for her." She looked at Barry with quiet conviction. "Some day we'll bring her home, Barry."

There were days when Analisa worked with her regular group at school and days when she went solely to visit Barry's daughter. Nearly fourteen now, the child was on the threshold of adulthood. Her hostility toward this young woman who visited so faithfully had diminished, and Beth now sometimes nodded or shook her head in response to Analisa's questions. One grey February day, feeling unaccountably restless, Analisa asked, "Do you like to walk on the beach, Beth?"

There was an unaccustomed gleam in her brown eyes as the young girl nodded with sudden vigor. "Daddy used to walk with me all the time. We'd take pictures and collect pretty shells."

Analisa caught her breath at the lovely, unexpected sound of the whispery voice and tried to suppress her wild elation. Her first intelligible words in over six years! But Analisa must remain nonchalant, pretend no miracle had happened lest the child should retreat, like a wild animal frightened by a sudden movement.

"Would you like to go with me today? It's a ragged, windy, wretched day, but I feel like matching mettle with the sea. Do you ever feel that way, Beth, as if you could whip the entire ocean to froth, shore to shore, with your own two hands?"

"Could we?" the soft voice begged.

"Could we!" Analisa could contain herself no longer. She caught the girl's hands and danced her around the room, and whether from exertion or from excitement, the first pink flush of color made Beth's face almost radiant. "Would you like your father to come with us?"

Instantly the pinkness faded, and suspicion clouded the eyes. "You know my father?" The shell was about to close over its prisoner once more. She had moved too fast. . . .

"I meet the parents of all my pupils and friends here," she said quickly, and was gratified by Beth's small scowl of reconsideration.

"I suppose it's all right, then."

Barry met them on the shore. "I have the loveliest surprise for you," Analisa had promised when she phoned him before she and her young charge had set out to walk the few blocks to the ocean's edge. "Please don't let your work keep you away—not even if you're photographing the Queen of England!"

Looming up out of the fog, he watched in disbelief as Analisa approached him, walking hand in hand with a small figure just out of reach of the waves. Heads bent against the chill, they weren't aware of him until he called out, "Analisa? *Beth?*" The child's head jerked upright, she quivered in fright for a moment, then tugged on Analisa's hand and pulled her forward.

Beth reached for her father's hand, her eyes luminous. "Daddy?" she ventured softly. "Walk with us?" She slipped her hand trustingly into his. It was their first physical contact in five years.

The three of them walked and talked and ran and finally grew tired, sharing a supper of pizza and hot chocolate. The fog had grown too thick to risk driving Beth back to her school, so Analisa arranged to keep her overnight. After an evening spent in quiet contemplation of Mozart, Beethoven and Bach, and a bit of country western to appease Beth's more prosaic tastes, Analisa lent the girl a too-long gown and tucked her up into her double bed—a performance from which Barry was barred, though later Beth let him come in to say good night. When Barry prepared to leave for his own flat, tears of gratitude were in his eyes. "I understand now why I couldn't take my eyes off you the first time I saw you," he said softly. "I looked into your eyes, and I saw my daughter. I saw the one person in the world who could touch her."

Analisa dressed for bed in the bathroom where she would not disturb her small guest, but when she slipped into the bedroom she was vexed to find the youngster sitting cross-legged in the middle of the bed, wide awake. "Where does my Daddy sleep when he doesn't sleep with you?" she demanded harshly. Violence simmered just beneath the surface, and Analisa knew a moment of fright before she forced herself to remain calmly matter-of-fact.

"He doesn't sleep with me, Beth, he sleeps in his own apartment. I'm sure he'd like to show you his house, if you'd ask him."

"You don't just know him because he's my dad. You know him better than that."

"I met your father about a month before I met you." She sat on the bed, refusing to be intimidated.

"Your father is married to your mother, and even though she has gone away, he has never, so far as I know, slept with anyone else. Certainly not with me."

"Never?"

"Never."

"Did Mama go away with—Ray?" Beth's huge eyes appealed for a denial, and Analisa swallowed hard. Never lie to a child. Never!

"I—I believe that's the name your father mentioned," she admitted.

"Ray!" Beth suddenly began to kick and scream, beating herself about the head and sobbing hysterically. "I'll kill him! I'll kill him!"

Helplessly Analisa let the child work the rage out of her system, and when Beth finally collapsed in a sobbing heap she cradled her in her arms and rocked her slowly. "Oh, my poor, hurting Beth," she crooned. "Please tell me what's hurting you so. Please let me help you stop hurting."

It was a patchy story, sobbed out between agonizing gulps. "I found them in b-bed, n-naked and he—he was on—on— Mama said if I ever told Daddy, he would k-kill us all. And R-R-Ray s-said—Mama had gone to the h-hairdressers, and I was sleeping in my room, and Ray c-came in and t-took off all his clothes and t-took off my gown and s-said he was going t-to show me what f-fun he and M-mama were h-having and then h-h-he—" Beth began to wail, and Analisa pulled her hard to her, burying the child's tear-streaked face against her shoulder.

"Beth, don't!" she pleaded. "Don't torment yourself. It was a despicable thing that he did, but it doesn't make you despicable or unworthy or any less of a wonderful, loyal child—"

"He said if I ever told anyone the three monkeys would come in the night and cut out my tongue and gouge out my eyes and pour hot lead in my ears! Don't tell anyone—*please* don't tell anyone, Analisa!"

Analisa held her silently a long while before deciding. "Ray can do none of those things. He was afraid, because he'd been so evil, and he silenced you by making you afraid, too. I think your father should know, Beth—he's older and wiser than we are. He'll know what to do, and he'll do whatever's best for you. He loves you so very much, and he's been unhappy because you've been unhappy. I think he'll want you to come live with him, and he'll prove to you that there are good men as well as bad ones in the world, just as there are good and bad women. You must not blame either yourself or all men or all grown-ups for what one man did."

CHAPTER 13

BARRY PRESSED her hand tightly when Analisa finished speaking, deeply distressed by her story. "Analisa," he asked softly, "if I get a special dispensation from the Church for a divorce, will you marry me?"

She shook her head regretfully. "No, Barry. I'm sure that under the circumstances the Church will grant you a divorce, so I think we should stop seeing one another. We *must* stop seeing each other now that you will be free to remarry."

"Do you really think it's that simple? Do you think I would ever forget you and learn to love another? As you have never forgotten . . . someone?"

"Yes. There has been no physical intimacy to make me unforgettable—" Too late she realized her error.

His pained eyes widened with the knowledge she had never meant to impart. "And was there with—him? Is that what happened to you?"

"Yes. I spent one night in his arms and I gave him—everything. What's left is not worth offering. Especially to you, who deserve so much more than I can ever give."

"And what about Beth? Is she to be abandoned again by someone she's come to love and trust?"

Analisa had been thinking about Beth too. "I'll still visit her, Barry, but you'll have to explain to her that I can never be your wife or her mother. I think you should begin dating others, so that when you are free she'll not miss me so keenly."

"By the time I'm free, perhaps you will be, too."

"No. I'll never be free, Barry." He kissed her on the mouth, a sorrowful kiss, and left her.

Although she often arranged to pick Beth up after school and entertain her, Analisa hadn't seen Barry for nearly three weeks when one afternoon he appeared on her doorstep. "I warned you I'd never give up trying to make a model of you," he explained, "and this is one assignment I will *not* let you refuse!" It was so good to see him again that Analisa let herself be persuaded as he draped a light sweater over her shoulders and led her to his car.

Her heart began to thud apprehensively as he found a parking spot near the top of Nob Hill, saying, "This job has to be done on location. They won't allow the props to leave the place." She walked along beside him, her hand moist in his. Nob Hill—how she had avoided this tourist mecca! For here was the San Francisco branch of de la Corte's Mother Lode. She had never dared run the risk of accidentally meeting Roan de la Corte or any of his associates.

The Mother Lode sign loomed ahead, and she stalled, admiring an expensive dress, a soft stole, and an elegant pair of Italian heels in a boutique window. She did not want to walk past that jewelry shop. A terrible foreboding gripped her. Innocently Barry pulled her along, his camera equipment heavy in his other hand, and to her horror, he led her not past the store but straight into it. Even in her distress, she noted that this establishment was not equal to the Scottsdale store—this sales room was much smaller, no more than a wide hallway sandwiched between the businesses on either side. The deep carpet was rose gold, the chairs were of a deeper, almost coppery gold brocade. The walls were striped in white satin and gold, and overhead lighting was recessed into the white ceiling. The glass tops and fronts of the showcases were as clear and shining as untouched crystal. She was still taking it all in when Barry pulled her attention back to his purpose in coming here.

"There!" he announced triumphantly, too pleased with his surprise to notice her reaction as he pointed to the necklace and earrings in a padlocked, shatterproof display case. "*The Analisa.* Now you see why I have to have you for my model!"

Analisa paled, and gripped her hands tightly behind her back, staring at the delicate chain of ivory bell-like blossoms of lily-of-the-valley with tiny gold clappers and stems and leaves of emerald. *May. It should have been emeralds,* Roan had said, and later he had given her a corsage of lily-of-the-valley because it was her birth flower. The gift Roan had been making for her twenty-second birthday, Trenton Westfield had hinted, would do well to be completed by her twenty-fourth one. And in a few weeks she would be twenty-four. . . .

Barry spoke to the impeccably attired salesman behind the counter, who proceeded to unlock the case and lift out the ensemble. "Undoubtedly among the finest pieces of jewelry in the world," he said, proffering the velvet box for Analisa's inspection, "to be sold only as a set." With shaking fingers, she lifted out the necklace and turned it over to look for the tiny engraved rearing horse that was Roan's logo. "TW," she murmured, puzzled and disappointed. "Trenton Westfield. I thought Roan—?"

Barry was watching her quizzically, aware for the first time of her pallor and trembling fingers. "Mr. Westfield executes all of Mr. de la Corte's designs," the salesman said stiffly, obviously taking offense at Analisa's presumption. To Barry he said, "We've arranged for you and the young lady to use the private showroom."

"He—I—" Analisa stammered, turning to Barry, "I'm not dressed for it. Roan prefers vignettes of head, shoulders, throat and jewels, with no distracting clothing—"

Barry stared at her incredulously. "Surely you wouldn't expect to pose in the—"

"Of course not!" she said sharply, then more gently, "Go ahead and set up your equipment. I know just the thing. I won't be a minute."

She hurried to the boutique and when Barry was ready for her, she presented herself in the soft, knitted stole she had admired, draped and tucked firmly about her bodice, revealing just a hint of cleavage. Her milky shoulders and throat were bare to receive the necklace which Barry clasped about her slender neck; her long hair was swept back and to one side, its retaining clip out of sight of the camera's eye, so that the life-size lily-of-the-valley earrings gleamed at her lobes. This was for Trenton, she persuaded herself, who had been her good friend—but she would never pose for anyone again.

Afterward, she refused Barry's invitation for coffee, because she had to be alone and because she couldn't bear to see the dawning, bewildered comprehension in his eyes. Alone in her apartment, she doubled with the pain of her lost love. If she had ever entertained any doubts, she knew now she could never marry Barry.

Late May was insufferably hot in Phoenix. Analisa stood beneath the airport's stylized mural of the great Phoenix bird risen from the ashes, awaiting the arrival of the other attendants on the flight to Denver and feeling grateful for the coolness of the air-conditioned terminal. The girl who had promised to replace her on the flight from San Francisco to Phoenix had come down with the flu shortly before departure time, and Analisa had been unable to avoid this trip. Immediately upon arrival, she had gone to her hotel room nearby, refusing to venture from it until it was time for her departing flight. Much as she longed to look once again upon Roan's beloved face, she would not seek him out or go to the Fifth Avenue shop.

She swung her gaze from her contemplation of the great mural—to find herself staring directly into Roan's startled grey eyes. He was entering the lobby with other arriving passengers, flight luggage in hand. Beneath his desert tan his face hardened as white as Italian marble. For one instant she thought he might approach her, speak; then she heard the rapid click of high heels on the tile floor and Luisa Costenza's high trilling voice. "Darling, I'm sorry I'm late." She deposited herself in Roan's arms, and in that moment Analisa escaped to the employee's lounge. When Roan looked up again, searching over Luisa's shoulder for the long-lost face, Analisa had vanished, a hallucination that had been as real as life.

Analisa huddled on the couch, curled up in agony. Her flight had already been called; she should have been on duty minutes ago. Two stewardesses from the latest arriving plane burst through the door, chattering happily. "What a dreamboat! I'd like to be in Costenza's negligee next month when she finally marries him."

"She's only been after Roan de la Corte for seven years. I think if it took me that long to break a man's resistance, I'd be looking elsewhere for a bit more enthusiasm."

Abruptly Analisa left her sanctuary and raced for her plane. Her trans-Atlantic circuit kept her away from San Francisco for more than a week, and when at last she checked off duty for a few days of freedom the dispatcher handed her an envelope. It was addressed in black type, sent in care of the airline office in Phoenix. There was no return address or postmark, and the duty officer told her the Phoenix personnel manager, taking hand delivery, had gone to the trouble of identifying Analisa's home base and sending it on.

In her apartment, Analisa opened the envelope with wildly shaking hands, to find inside another envelope, this one addressed in her father's familiar handwriting to Roan's Carefree address. The post date, she noted, indicated it probably had arrived at his home within hours of her precipitate departure more than two years ago. Strange that Roan should have kept the letter all this time, let alone bother to send it on. Now that he could find her, why had he not brought it to her himself? But of course he was being married soon. . . .

"Little One," she read with blurred eyes, "I've been drying out for some time now, and I'm sober today. I hope it will last, though I don't say it will—I've never been a strong-willed person, and without your wonderful mother's iron-in-velvet influence, I seem not to be of much substance. This is what I want to say to you: Roan de la Corte is. Don't castigate him for taking you from me. At the time I was trying to find the courage and the means to send you away without alarming you, for my creditors had already warned me what would happen to you if I failed to pay. So you see, I have wronged you as abominably as I wronged your mother. What Roan is doing is for your own safety, out of the greatness and fearlessness of his heart. Or maybe out of love in his heart, for I'm sure he has not acted without personal risk . . ." There were a few more shaky half-legible words, but Analisa didn't attempt to decipher them. They were all so wrong and so long dead! How could her father consider Roan a hero, when surely his blood ties to the Costenza faction alone gave him immunity from danger? Roan de la Corte had taken what he wanted, had plucked the fruit and discarded the hull. . . . It was all part of the past, she must put it behind her. She crumpled the letter and tossed it into the incinerator.

She bathed and dressed carefully, and then consulted her watch. Beth would still be in school; unless he was out on assignment, Barry should be at his studio. She was feeling dreadfully, dreadfully alone, terrifyingly near, once again, to the end of all hope.

Barry sat at his desk comparing two photos. When she entered, he laid them face down and looked up at her with bleak eyes that betrayed lack of sleep.

"You're back," he said flatly. The words startled her, because he had not contacted her in all the weeks since she had modeled Roan's—no, Trenton Westfield's—jewelry. But even more disturbing were the resignation in his voice, the lack of warmth in his brown eyes.

"I didn't think you'd miss me," she began uncertainly, and to her annoyance she found herself nervously opening and closing the clasp of her handbag.

"I expect I'll spend the rest of my life missing you, Analisa."

Hesitantly, she whispered, "I came to ask if you—if you would still consider accepting—a part of a woman?"

Not a muscle in his face moved. His eyes were deeply unreadable as he sat staring at her, and she stood immobile, her hands now quietly gripping her bag.

"No," he said at last. "Not a part of a woman, with a ghost lying between us at night."

He turned the two photos face up on his desk, and Analisa gasped softly. Beside the vignette he himself had made, with Analisa's coppery-gold hair and creamy skin set against a black background, the perfect foil for the ivory, gold and emerald jewels, was the turquoise-grounded photograph taken in Roan's office nearly three years before. "I finally realized where I'd seen you before. This photo . . . I remember there was some talk at the time, cruel gossip. . . ." He seemed discursive, unable to settle to any one thought. He touched one photo, then the other, commenting regretfully, "In the one, looking cherished and virginal and infinitely desirable; in the other, possessed and—*dis*possessed. And more desirable than any woman has the right to be—" He looked at her, and his eyes sharpened. "You were right to say there was not enough left to give to another man. No whole man could live with it. Whatever happened, Analisa, you still belong to him. Go back to him and make it work!" His voice had risen, the anger slicing finely across his despairing face failing to disguise his underlying anguish.

She shook her head. "It's too late. He's marrying Luisa Costenza in June." She consulted her calendar watch automatically. "It's June already, isn't it?" She shrugged. "I'm sorry to have offered you seconds, Barry. Forgive me. Let's, for Beth's sake, remain friends." She started to turn away without his answer.

"Analisa!" The sharpness in his voice brought her about. "Don't you ever cry?" He regarded her in utter, wet-eyed misery, and she returned his stare, her own eyes hard and bright as fever.

"No, Barry. I never cry." She turned and walked soundlessly from the room.

Analisa was relieved when June ended. She need no longer ask, "Has he married her yet?" It was by now a *fait accompli*. But the certainty of it was even more crushing than her assumption, during all the previous months, that Roan had married Luisa as quickly as he'd been able to rid himself of Analisa.

The flight was progressing smoothly, and she sat in the lounge, smartly nyloned legs crossed to reveal slim ankles and curvaceous calves, idly flipping through a new *Vogue* magazine. Suddenly she found herself face to face with her own image, wearing the Analisa necklace and earrings. "Analisa" was the only caption to the tasteful advertisement, followed in small script by "de la Corte's Mother Lode, San

Francisco or Scottsdale." Did she really look like
that? Looking at the photograph objectively, she saw
strength in the fine facial bones, shadows of sadness
beneath ocean-green eyes, and generosity and gentleness in a mouth that tried to smile. Ten years
from now, what sort of picture would stare back at
her? That of a harsh-faced, thin-lipped, dry-eyed
spinster who had tasted the bitterest dregs of life and
had long ago forsaken the catharsis of tears?

She stared at the jewels. Roan's design, once intended as a birthday gift. Nothing would ever convince her otherwise. Yet it had been Trenton
Westfield who had ultimately executed the design,
when Roan had abandoned it to more satisfying pur-
suits. Her heart contracted painfully. Was there a
message here for her? Could Trenton have found
that Polly Austen was not the one for him after all?
No! She could not think that there had ever been
anything between herself and Trenton Westfield
other than sincere mutual respect and friendship.
But Roan's public denouncement had condemned
Trent as much as herself. Could Polly have got word
of it and not understood after all? Perhaps she had
called off the engagement? The troubling thought
left her doubly damned.

She was glad when the flight ended. Forgoing her
usual cup of coffee with one or another of her
crewmates, Analisa headed for the sanctuary of her
quiet apartment. She bathed in scented water and
changed into turquoise satin lounging pajamas with
wide legs and a square-necked tunic top. Except for
the smart gold watch at her wrist and the plain gold
clip she sometimes wore in her hair, she never wore
jewelry of any kind. Memories were too potent. Tonight, she left her hair loose, a fan about her shoul-

ders that shimmered from gold to copper depending upon the lighting where she moved. She put several classical tapes on the stereo and lay back forlornly on the couch, remembering the serene evenings she and Barry had spent in this room. He had assiduously avoided her for months, and gradually he had been weaning Beth away from her, too. No use yearning for the impossible—Roan was long gone now—but she couldn't help wishing that Barry had not taken her so literally when she'd suggested they should part. What she had suggested, in fact, had been a gradual easing of their relationship, not the abrupt amputation he seemed to have chosen on the day she had modeled for him. She was totally alone again. And frightened. She buried her face in her hands and wished for the cathartic tears that would never fall, and it was a while before she became aware that the doorbell was ringing insistently.

She opened the door and found herself confronted by white-faced fury—beneath wavy brown hair, dark brown eyes as shocked as her own must have been; a neatly trimmed beard; thin, angry lips. Long fingers clenching a magazine waved before her eyes, to display the head and shoulders of a girl wearing only a haunting expression and exquisite jewelry.

"Trenton!"

He pushed past her, not waiting for an invitation, then slammed the door behind him and leaned heavily against it. "My God! We thought you were dead! You were right to run when you did, but why in *hell* did you never come back?"

"Come back to what, Trent?" Then, gathering her thoughts, she asked quickly, "Where's Polly? How did you find me? What are you doing in San Francisco?"

He smiled at last, his face momentarily relaxing. "Polly wanted to come home for her first confinement so her mother can look after her when she leaves the hospital. Our daughter was born," he glanced proudly at his watch, "exactly one hour and twenty-seven minutes ago."

Then, remembering his mission, he waved the magazine again and stepped farther into the room. "It was while I was chewing my nails in the hospital that I started putting two and two together. Barry Marcus is a San Francisco photographer, so I started making some calls. It was worse than a fist in the gut, you flaunting our jewelry after letting us believe all these months—years—that you were dead—"

She shook her head. "And why should I be dead? Roan, at least, knows better. We had an inadvertent encounter some weeks ago at the Phoenix airport. He saw me as clearly as I saw him. And Luisa."

Trenton's mouth dropped open. "When exactly was this?" His eyes narrowed intently.

"On my birthday, to be exact."

He sucked in his breath. "May twenty-eighth. The day Roan chose to break his engagement to Luisa. He never was very keen about marrying her, so I didn't attach any significance to it when he broke it off."

"He—isn't married?" A flicker ignited in her eyes, then quickly died. "He forwarded a letter to me that my father wrote two years ago. If a letter could find me, then so could he. He chose not to. Don't lay his broken romance at my feet, Trent. He didn't come to me because he doesn't want me. He's obviously still a . . . a trifler."

The brown eyes opened wide with incredulity. "Do

191

you really believe his pride would let him come, after—"

"Pride!" she cried out in exasperation. "What has pride to do with love?" Her passion deflated, and she ended lamely, "But he never loved me, did he? It was only I who loved him."

Trenton threw the magazine to the floor and grasped her shoulders, shaking her in vexation. "If you love him, Analisa, and if *your* pride can take the buffeting, then go to him. Go now! Tonight!"

"Will he have me?"

He released her and ran a hand through his thick brown hair. "I don't know, Analisa. If he won't, he's a fool who deserves to die of his misery—or to live with it."

She looked at him quizzically, and he felt a shiver run the length of his spine. "It's possible to do both at the same time, you know," she said quietly, and then refusing to explain, she ushered him out the door, bade him deliver her love to Polly, and began throwing things willy-nilly into an overnight bag.

Ignoring the astonished salesmen, Analisa raced down the corridor toward Roan's private office before she could lose the momentum of her courage. A clerk, new since her time, moved a hand to activate some sort of signal. The alarm must have reached Roan, for when she burst in on him, he was sitting behind his desk, his left hand reaching into the top drawer for a gun. "Roan," she whispered softly, leaning weakly against the closed door behind her. Excitement and apprehension lent color to her high-boned cheeks, and her eyes were a luminous green, beseeching.

Roan's grey eyes were startled for only an instant

before anger began to glint in them like sun on a steel blade. She was slender, vulnerable, more beautiful than ever. Staring, he sat rigid, his left hand arrested on its way to the gun in the drawer, the other out of sight behind the desk. "What right have you to barge in here? The staff knows better than to permit strangers beyond—"

"They didn't permit me," she protested softly, moving toward him, "and we weren't always strangers. Roan, please listen to me—"

"Listen to you!" he said savagely. "I waited months to listen to you. It's much too late now."

Her feet dragged to a halt a few feet from his desk. Her eyes searched the virile, handsome face, not a single precious detail forgotten, the pulsing jaw, the lacerating eyes that always could make or break her. "Is it pride," she implored, "or do you really hate me?"

A deep, impenetrable shaft of emotion briefly pierced his eyes, and then the angry mask was quickly back in place. "Hate you?" he sneered. "My God, how I hate you! I thought you were dead. I was free. I wish you'd stayed that way!"

"Do you?" From somewhere, steely calm overcame her, and her face and voice became impassive. "I almost did." She spun on her heel and retraced her steps to the door. Behind her, the desk drawer slammed shut so sharply she flinched, imagining the sound of a gun.

"Analisa. Was there a child?" His voice was quiet now, washing over the turbulence of his emotion of a moment ago. "Or did you destroy that too?"

She turned to face him defiantly, tears in her eyes, her hand on the doorknob. He was standing behind his desk, leaning his weight on clumped fists, his eyes searing hers. Those hands that had always been at rest, no matter how violent the emotions inside the man, were now tight-clenched to hold to his pride and his rage and his contempt.

Her lips parted soundlessly as she stared at him in anguished longing and disbelief. At last, she got the words out, gently, her voice steady despite the upheaval in her heart. "They said there wasn't one, Roan." She wrenched the door open and was gone before he could see the bereavement in her eyes, the shattering impact of her need for this one man who hated her so unforgivingly.

"Analisa!" The angry word cannonaded down the hall after her, but her feet had set their course. She didn't stop, didn't slow, wouldn't let herself think or feel until she was safely on her plane bound for San Francisco.

CHAPTER 14

ANALISA brought an angled first-feeder sterling spoon for week-old Lisa Westfield, and for the new mother a bouquet of pink roses and baby's breath. She had deliberately waited a few days before visiting Polly to ensure that Trenton would already have taken himself and his questions back to Phoenix. To her dismay, he was sitting in the nursery, his rosy-faced daughter on his lap, examining with delight the pink perfection of her tiny fingers. "The hands of an artist, if ever I saw any!" he exulted, and then looked up, disconcerted to see that it was not his wife's shadow that had fallen across the object of his examination.

"I thought you'd be back in Phoenix by now," Analisa apologized, trying to remember how to smile.

"I thought *you'd* be in Phoenix now!" The sharpness of his voice startled the baby on his lap, who set up a distressed howl, and impulsively Analisa reached for her, cuddling and soothing her before laying her in the pink-and-white rocking cradle. "Why didn't you take my advice?" he asked grimly.

"I went." She tucked a sheet about the drowsy baby, and saw that Polly had come to stand in the

195

doorway with the flowers in water, looking flushed and happily maternal in her long cotton dressing gown. Analisa looked back at the baby and said matter-of-factly, "He said he'd rather I was dead." A signal must have passed between husband and wife, for Polly turned without a word and left them alone.

Trenton's eyes narrowed. "And you let it go at that?"

"What would you have done? Fallen to your knees and kissed his hands?"

"Unequivocally—*yes!*" he said. "Why did you give up so easily?"

"The more I love him, the more it hurts. I just can't endure any more of his hate, Trenton, I just can't." She sank to her heels before him, her hands pressed to her face, shoulders convulsing with her tearless, racking grief. "I wish—oh, I wish I could return to that oblivion where nothing ever hurts."

Strong hands grasped her shoulders. "What are you saying, Analisa? What happened to you when you left us? Where did you go?"

Half-coherently the words tumbled out. The devastation she had felt when Roan had so cruelly denounced and dismissed her; the yellow car that had followed and terrorized her; her rage against Roan's baby and her subsequent desolation when she learned it had miscarried; the peaceful months when she'd curled, mindless, without history or future, on the hard straw pallet of the isolated mountain refuge. Trenton listened in stunned silence. When she'd finished talking, he leaned forward earnestly, hands clasped between his knees, his eyes boring intently into hers.

"I could intercede for you, but I'm not going to. You and Roan will have to make your own way. But you deserve to know what you're up against. At least some of it—some things you'll have to learn for yourself." He paused, seeming to wonder how to begin, and then began at the beginning. "When Roan paid your father's gambling debt, his only thought was to protect you. Maybe he was already in love with you then, or maybe, as a connoisseur of beautiful things, he just couldn't bear to think what gangsters might do to that perfect face." He paused. "I do know that by the time I came on the scene, he was half insane with love for you."

He was silent a long time, as if letting that sink in. "The car that almost hit you in front of the shop when Roan was in New York, the arrow lodged inches above your head—did you really think two such accidents could be coincidental? They were deadly warnings. The yellow car might have turned out to be more than a warning had you not eluded them. Roan had something they wanted—and it was *that*, or *you*."

She rocked back on her heels. Terror flooded her face. "That accursed Rachmaninoff Emerald!"

"Yes, the emerald. Someone wanted it—and they bargained for it with your face. You were their bait because Roan cared. But he wouldn't deal, and Rachmaninoff would neither sell him the emerald nor let him renege on his contract—though in the end, he had to. Nobody will touch that emerald, and today it is a museum piece under heavy guard. To protect you, to prove his lack of interest in you, Roan openly dated other women—numerous women for to favor one would make that one their next piece of live bait.

"That night I came back for the rest of my things, Roan's vile accusations were part of a plan, the first step of preparing your responses for when he would finally be forced to drive you out of his life. He had waited outside the house for hours that night, knowing I intended to drop by, but he had not yet taken me into his confidence. I was as outraged as you were hurt. But later, those dates you and I had were a part of Roan's scheme to convince his enemies that there was nothing between you and him. Only he and I and Polly knew the truth—though Polly, for her own peace of mind, was fed no more than minimal information.

"When it came to the final showdown, even I thought he was unnecessarily brutal. He wasn't, Analisa. He had heard through the Costenza grapevine—it is in their best interests to keep track of all rival organizations' activities—that the jewel thieves were going to move that day. Two of their men, charged with making sure your face didn't come unscarred through the day, were planted in the restaurant when Roan confronted us."

Analisa finally spoke. "So he sent me away, so humiliated and degraded that no one, least of all I, could ever believe he didn't hate me. But if he cared for me then, why does he hate me so much now?"

"Because you didn't come back, Analisa. When he needed you as much as you've ever needed him, you didn't come back. When the conspirators were caught in a trap of their own making and were gunned down by Costenza's men, Roan was finally free of that emerald curse and you were safe and free to return. When your father died a few weeks later and still no word came from you, we could only assume that they had got to you after all, and that you were dead. It took Roan a long time to deal with that. Then when he finally accepted it and tried to return to a normal life with marriage to Luisa, I gather you rose like the phoenix from the ashes to haunt him again. I wonder if you can ever know what it cost him to send you away, only to learn that you hadn't cared enough to come back when he needed you? But I'm convinced that if he didn't love you still, Analisa, he would have gone ahead with his marriage to Luisa. Go home, dearest girl, and don't accept hate for an answer."

The night was muggy and the stars overhead seemed to shimmer in a haze of heat. After San Francisco, the Arizona heat soaked up Analisa's energy like a sponge. She parked her rented car a quarter of a mile from the house, just off the Carefree-Scottsdale road, and walked quietly off the edge of the driveway to avoid the crunch of gravel beneath her feet. Except for a pale patch of light lying across the patio outside Roan's room, the house was in darkness. Her heart thumping painfully, she picked her way carefully and silently through the desert scrub toward the light. She feared that if she rang the doorbell, Roan would only close the door in her face, so she stood uncertainly against the corner of the house, shielded by creosote and ocotillo until her eyes adjusted and focused on the accoutrements of the shadowy poolside deck. The lounges were empty, but on the small round table stood a full shot glass, a liquor bottle and a metal ashtray with a cigarette balanced on the edge from which rose a straight column of smoke. Since Roan neither smoked nor drank, it could only mean he had a guest. She moved forward cautiously, reluctant to see what might be going on in that dimly lit bedroom, but resolved not to leave without at least trying to effect a reconciliation, even if it meant waiting out here all night.

Over the waterfall she could hear nothing. It was difficult to see into the room beyond the yellow glow of the lamps burning on each side of the closed sliding doors. The wrought iron grille was not locked, as she had feared it might be, but she couldn't just barge in. Better to wait until he sent his guest home . . . if he did. There had been no car standing in the drive, which meant she would have to be taken home—unless she was meant to remain for the night. Already defeated, Analisa crept around the pool to the far side of the flagstone deck and huddled back among the tumbled boulders to wait.

A dim light went on in the bedroom, but from her position behind the rocks she could see nothing of the interior except the wide cherrywood dresser that backed against the bathroom wall.

Presently Roan came alone to stand at the pool's edge, staring unseeingly into the moonless night. With his back to the light, shadows disguised his features, except for an occasional metallic glint in his grey eyes. With his hands dug deep into the pockets of his long red robe, his shoulders defiantly squared, he looked regal—and forsaken. Listlessly, he reached down for the smouldering cigarette with his left hand and raised it to inhale heavily, its glowing tip flaring to reveal lines of pain in his face. He exhaled, then lifted the shot glass from the table, swallowing its contents at a single gulp. *Oh, no, Roan! With your need of a steady hand and discerning eye! Not Daddy's way, not that!* She wanted to run to him, to throw herself into his arms, to tell him how much he mattered to her. She sat riveted to the rocks, unable to move. To her relief, he downed only the one shot, took only a couple of puffs before impatiently crushing out the cigarette and returning to his room. Now was the time to act, before he could close and lock the iron gate, but she was too unnerved to move. Inching forward, she could see Roan standing immobile in the center of the room, his ravaged face no longer a carefully prepared mask, staring with deep absorption at the wall above his bed. She saw him move toward the hallway connecting his room to what had been her own, saw a flash of bright light quickly extinguished as he entered the bathroom and closed the door.

She scrambled from her hiding place and hurried across the flagstones, pushing aside the sliding glass door and stepping into the air-conditioned comfort of his room. Only one light burned now, above the bed, and crossing to where Roan had stood, she turned to see what had held him so still for so long.

She gasped. Her own likeness looked down on her, filling the space above the bed—Barry Marcus's triumphant capturing of Analisa in the lily-of-the-valley necklace and earrings, spotlighted by a single light expertly trained upon the picture to wash away all shadows.

"A tortured angel, wouldn't you say?" mocked a soft, timbrous voice behind her, "paying the price of faithlessness. Why did you come back, Analisa? Without your child, I have no need of you."

She whirled, her eyes bright with pain. He stood as he had stood on the patio, feet braced apart, hands in pockets, eyes afire, his proud head held at a regal angle. "You *do* have need of me!" she cried. "You still need your child. *I* need your child!"

His hands tensed in his pockets, and a muscle throbbed whitely in his jaw as he enunciated each venomous word distinctly, "You didn't come back when I needed you, and I don't need you now."

"But *I* need *you!* Roan, can't you understand? *I love you!*" She turned and motioned helplessly toward the portrait over his bed. "That's not a tortured angel, Roan. That's a tortured human being who has never stopped hearing the most beloved voice in the world condemning her to hell on earth." She turned to face him again, acutely aware of the nearness of his lean, muscular body. "This morning, Trenton told me why you did it—"

His hands came out of his pockets, swift as rapiers, to imprison her face. "*What* did he tell you?"

Swift as the movement had been, she had seen the ridged protrusions on his right hand—the hand that, had she but been alert, she'd have realized he'd kept concealed, reaching for a gun in his desk with his left one, smoking his cigarette, raising the glass to his lips.

"Roan! Your hand—" He tried to replace it quickly in his pocket, but she caught and held it, staring in sick horror at the smashed, knobby bones that had not mended properly. *Mr. Westfield executes all of Mr. de la Corte's designs.* How could she ever have comprehended the rebuke in the salesman's voice! An anguished sob broke from her lips. "You sent me away and offered yourself as the bait in my place." She kissed the maimed hand, and suddenly all her stored tears spilled over onto it, scalding it. "Why, Roan, why? It should have been me, not you! What good is a beautiful face that gains one nothing, when your hands are so precious!"

He stood unyielding, his mouth drawn in a hard line. "I don't need your pity, Analisa."

She lifted her head defiantly. "I'm not offering you pity, Roan. I'm offering you myself. I'm offering you children to carry on the work that you've been denied. You don't have to marry me, Roan. You don't have to love me or even to like me. But please let me stay with you." She was begging with all her heart as he'd once said she would.

"What kind of man do you think I am?" he raged, jerking his hand savagely from her and almost throwing her off balance.

She stared at him levelly, and pity did creep into her features. "A wounded man, Roan. As wounded— but *no more wounded*—than I." She looked at him for a long moment, then turned and walked to the door. Her hand on the handle, head bowed, she said without turning to look at him, "I'd rather have a bludgeoned face than a bludgeoned heart, Roan."

She had the door open when his voice, emotionless yet compelling, halted her. "Analisa. Don't walk through that door." She stood for long seconds before turning slowly, her face impassive, to assess the plea in his suddenly vulnerable eyes. "Don't ever leave me again, Analisa."

Slowly his plea penetrated her numbed mind, and a joyous light leaped into her face as hope lifted her heart. They came together in the center of the room, Roan's hands caressing her hair, her lovely face, looking into the sea-green eyes that would always carry in their depths the memory of her suffering, just as his hand would always bear the injury he had sustained in her place. He teased her trembling mouth with his lips, and she tasted his kiss, clinging to him.

"What became of the baby that according to all the evidence we should have had?" he quizzed tenderly, and she blushed like a schoolgirl.

"I—I didn't realize you kept such close track of me."

"I was always aware of everything about you, darling. Everything." The sensuality in his voice sent desire curling through her, and she pressed closer to him, delighting in his need of her.

For a moment he held her away and searched her eyes. "What did you mean when I asked about a child and you said, 'They said there wasn't one'? I was so sure you'd bring my child back to me once you learned the danger was over. When my hand was smashed in retaliation for my refusal to surrender the Rachmaninoff Emerald, it created worldwide reaction. You couldn't have been unaware of it, yet—"

She leaned back against the arm that encircled her waist and stopped the words with her hand, looking up earnestly into his face. "No one was ever more loved, more needed than you, Roan. When I left here, I had no place to go, no one to love; my life had come to an end. I had an accident and collapsed at the hideout of a Mexican refugee family who took me in until I recovered. I was ill for months, unable to dress or feed myself, unable to think or remember my name. They said—I lost the baby. Then I learned I'd lost my father, too. You had sent me away in hatred, and there was no going back, so I went on. I managed to avoid every flight to Phoenix but the one, because I couldn't bear being so near and not seeing you. I love you so, I couldn't face your hatred again."

"Then I really saw you—you weren't just a hallucination reminding me that I could never marry another woman?" He gathered her possessively close. She could feel the heat of his body, the tautness of his muscles, the driving male need that sent desire flooding through her until she felt as if she were drenched in liquid fire. He touched his lips to the pounding pulse at her throat, murmuring, "Your need is my need. My darling, loving me so, why did you run away that day?"

"Because Luisa was in your arms. One of the stewardesses from your flight said your wedding would take place in a few days. Roan, I wanted to die."

"And I think a big part of me did die the day I sent you away." He held up his injured hand. "This was nothing compared to the pain of cutting my heart out, knowing that our hearts were so closely intertwined you would suffer my pain, as I suffered yours. My darling, never, never leave me again."

"Never," she whispered, spreading his lapels to smooth her palms over his hard chest and feel the beat of his heart. She smiled shyly up at him and lifted her face for his kiss. "You once told me I'd have to beg. I'm begging, Roan."

She lifted her arms to him, offering herself unashamedly. He swept her into his arms and carried her to the bed. Slowly he began to undress her, caressing her body with every practiced movement of his hands until she lay naked and eager beneath his adoring gaze.

Unbelting his robe and tossing it aside, he lowered his body to hers and dipped his head to taste the sweetness of her. His hand sought the switch of the spotlight that illuminated her picture above the bed. "I don't need that tonight," he murmured against her lips, "now I've got the real girl."

THE AVON ROMANCE

RANSOMED HEART
April 1983

SPARKY ASCANI

A lovely young woman offers to sell her jewelry to pay her father's gambling debts but the buyer, a dashing jewelry designer, will accept nothing less than the most precious jewel of all—Analisa! The twosome must overcome separation and danger before Analisa's ransomed heart is free to love.   83287-9/$2.95

NOW COMES THE SPRING
May 1983

ANDREA EDWARDS

Adventurous, creative newspaper photographer Tracy Monroe agrees to pose as the fiancee of cool, tough-talking star reporter Josh Rettinger because he can't face Christmas with his family alone. But their role playing becomes more than make-believe, offering them unexpected feelings of desire…and a passion that brings the warmth of spring.   83329-8/$2.95

AVON Paperbacks

Available wherever paperbacks are sold or directly from the publisher. Include 50¢ per copy for postage and handling: allow 6-8 weeks for delivery. Avon Books, Mail Order Dept., 224 W. 57th St., N.Y., N.Y. 10019